Bubble Gum
Rescue

Candy Fairies

Bubble Gum Rescue

HELEN PERELMAN

ILLUSTRATED BY
ERICA-JANE WATERS

ALADDIN
NEW YORK LONDON TORONTO SYDNEY NEW DELHI

ALADDIN

An imprint of Simon & Schuster Children's Publishing Division

1230 Avenue of the Americas, New York, NY 10020

First Aladdin paperback edition July 2012

Text copyright © 2012 by Helen Perelman

Illustrations copyright © 2012 by Erica-Jane Waters

All rights reserved, including the right of reproduction in whole or in part in any form.

ALADDIN is a trademark of Simon & Schuster, Inc., and related logo is a registered
trademark of Simon & Schuster, Inc.

For information about special discounts for bulk purchases, please contact
Simon & Schuster Special Sales at 1-866-506-1949 or business@simonandschuster.com.

The Simon & Schuster Speakers Bureau can bring authors to your live event.

For more information or to book an event, contact the Simon & Schuster
Speakers Bureau at 1-866-248-3049 or visit our website at www.simonspeakers.com.

Designed by Karina Granda

The text of this book was set in Berthold Baskerville Book.

Manufactured in the United States of America 0814 OFF

4 6 8 10 9 7 5 3

Library of Congress Control Number 2011934219

ISBN 978-1-4424-2217-9

ISBN 978-1-4424-2218-6 (eBook)

For Elle Dean Brown,
a choc-o-rific reader at P. S. 6 in NYC

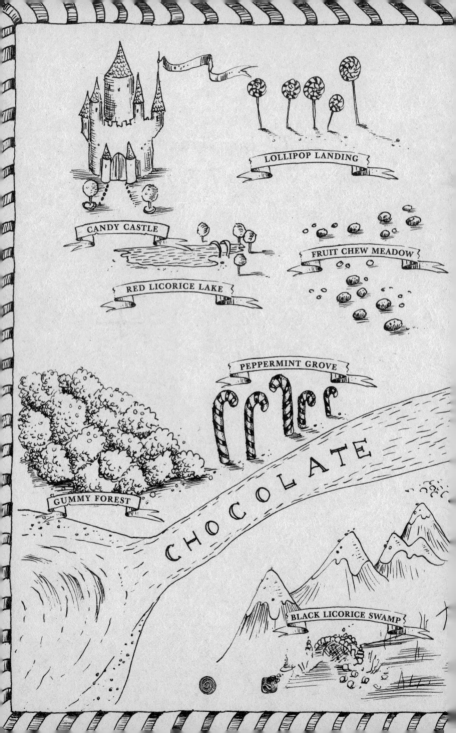

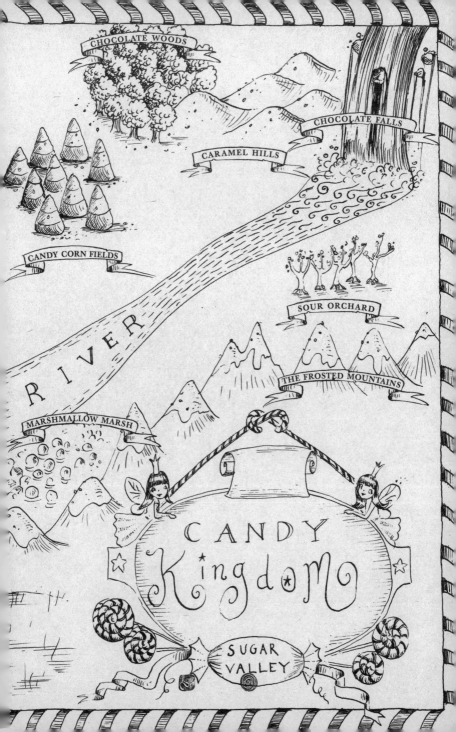

Contents

CHAPTER
1

A Sticky Mess

Early in the morning, Melli the Caramel Fairy flew to the top of Caramel Hills. She was checking on the caramel chocolate rolls she had made with her Chocolate Fairy friend Cocoa. Melli smiled at their newest creation drying in the cool shade of a caramel tree. Yesterday the two fairies had worked hard rolling small logs of caramel and then dipping them in chocolate. The final touch was a drizzle of butterscotch on top. Melli couldn't wait to taste one!

A caramel turtle jutted his head out of his shell and smelled the fresh candy. Melli laughed. "You were hiding over by that log," she said to the turtle. She kneeled down next to him. "Did you think you'd snatch a candy without my noticing?"

The turtle quickly slipped his head back into his shell. Still as a rock, he waited to see what the Caramel Fairy would do.

Melli placed one of the candies in front of him. "Of course you may have one," she said sweetly. "There's enough to share."

The turtle stuck his head out again and gobbled it up.

"Do you like the candy?" Melli asked.

The turtle nodded, and Melli smiled. "Cocoa and I are going to bring these to Sun Dip this evening," she said.

Sun Dip was the time at the end of the day when the sun set behind the Frosted Mountains and the Candy Fairies relaxed. Melli loved visiting with her friends and catching up on everyone's activities. And today she and Cocoa would bring their new candy. She hoped her friends would enjoy the sweet treat.

Just as Melli was putting the candies in her basket, she heard a squeal. It sounded like an animal in trouble. She put the basket down and walked toward the sound.

"Hot caramel!" Melli cried as she peered around one of the caramel trees.

Lying on the ground was a small caramella bird. He was trying to flap his wings to fly, but they were barely moving. Melli leaned in closer and noticed that the bird's feathers were wet and stuck together.

Melli reached out to the bird. "You poor thing," she whispered. She tried to calm the little one by talking to him. Caramella birds lived in the valley of Caramel Hills and had bright yellow wing feathers. They lived off the seeds of the caramel trees and filled the hills with their soft chirps.

"Where have you been playing?" Melli asked sweetly. She carefully picked up the bird and gently stroked his head. Immediately she realized that his feathers were covered in thick butterscotch. "How did you get coated in this syrup?" she asked. "No wonder you can't move or fly."

The bird chirped loudly. It was shaking in her hands.

"Butterscotch is not the best thing for feathers," Melli said, smiling at the tiny caramella. "Don't worry, sweetie," she added softly. "Let's give you a good bath and get this mess off your wings. I know all about sticky caramel." She patted the bird's head gently. "I will get you cleaned up in no time. Let's go to the water well and rinse you off."

Melli held on to the bird and flew to the edge of Caramel Hills. The tiny creature seemed to relax in Melli's hands, but his heart was still pounding. At the well Melli began to wash the butterscotch off the bird's wings. She knew she'd have to spend some time scrubbing. She had gotten caramel on her clothes before, and it often took a while to get all the goo off.

After a few rinses Melli began to see his brightly colored feathers.

"There, that does it," she said, feeling satisfied. She stood back and looked at the little bird. "You do have gorgeous yellow wings!"

The bird shook the water off his wings. He was happy to be able to move them freely. He bowed his head to Melli, thanking her for helping him.

"You should be able to fly now," Melli said. "Be careful, and stay away from the sticky stuff!"

"Hi, Melli!" Cocoa appeared next to her. "What are you doing here?"

"Cocoa," Melli gasped. "You scared me! I didn't see you there." She pointed to the caramella bird.

"Look who I found. He was covered in butter-scotch, and his wings were stuck together. I just gave him a bath with the fresh well water."

Cocoa's wings fluttered. "Oh, bittersweet chocolate," she said sadly. "This is worse than I thought."

"What are you talking about?" Melli asked. "He's all clean now. He'll be able to fly."

"It's not only this bird I am worried about," Cocoa said. "I heard from a sugar fly that there was a butterscotch syrup spill on the eastern side of Butterscotch Volcano. That must be where this one got syrup on his wings. *All* the cara-mella birds are in danger!"

"Oh no," Melli said. "So many caramella birds live over there. What else did the sugar fly tell you?"

"That was all," Cocoa replied.

Sugar flies passed information around Sugar Valley. If a fairy wanted to get the word out about something important, the sugar flies were the ones to spread the news.

"Let's go now," Melli said urgently. "If Butterscotch Volcano erupts, there'll be a large spill in the hills." She looked down at the bird. "Is that what happened to you? Will you take us to where you got butterscotch on your wings?"

The bird took flight, and Melli and Cocoa trailed after him. His yellow feathers gleamed in the sunlight. Melli beat her wings faster. She was very concerned about what kind of sticky mess they were going to find.

CHAPTER

2

Butterscotch Volcano

Melli grabbed Cocoa's hand. She couldn't believe the sight below her. Butterscotch Volcano was in the middle of Caramel Hills, and a place where Caramel Fairies often gathered. Once a year at the Butterscotch Festival, a few brave and experienced Caramel Fairies would dip into the volcano for a supply of hot butterscotch.

The extra-sweet syrup was then stored in large barrels in Candy Castle and used throughout the year for special candy projects.

Melli's eyes widened as she saw the thick syrup pooled in the large area east of the volcano. The land was flat, and the caramella birds built their nests there. Now it was a lake of syrupy butterscotch. Melli shook her head in disbelief. Never before had she seen butterscotch ooze out of the volcano. While there was hot butterscotch syrup deep within the volcano, there had not been an eruption in a long, long time.

As Melli flew over the volcano with Cocoa she squeezed her friend's hand tighter. "No wonder that little bird got his feathers sticky," Melli said. She pointed down below—butterscotch was *everywhere*!

"The sugar flies were definitely right about this," Cocoa said. "This is a supersticky mess."

"Did you send the sugar fly to Raina, Berry, and Dash?" Melli asked. If things were this bad, she wanted all her friends to know. Together, the five of them could work to help the caramella birds of Caramel Hills.

Cocoa nodded. "Yes, I sent them each a message," she replied. "I hope they can get here fast."

Melli carefully observed the area. "Look, Cocoa, the butterscotch isn't coming from the *top* of the volcano," she said. She pointed to the top, which was clean and dry. "Where do you think it's coming from?"

Cocoa squinted and then flapped her golden wings. "Let's get a better look," she said bravely.

The two friends flew down closer to the volcano. The sight broke Melli's heart.

"The poor birds," Melli said softly. "This is their home, and now it's a sticky, syrupy mess. "

"They can't even move," Cocoa added. She saw many birds trying to flap their butterscotch-coated wings.

As Melli looked around she suddenly spotted her sister, Cara, perched on a caramel tree. "There's Cara," she said. "Maybe she knows what's going on."

Cara was rubbing a small bird's feathers with a sponge. She was dipping the sponge in a pail of water when Melli and Cocoa landed next to her.

"Oh, Melli!" Cara exclaimed. "I'm so happy you came! We need all the help we can get. This spill is spreading fast."

"How did this happen?" Melli asked. She knelt down next to her sister.

"The volcano cracked, and there's a leak on its side," Cara explained. "I heard the older Caramel Fairies talking."

"Bittersweet," Cocoa muttered.

"All this butterscotch is oozing out of the volcano?" Melli gasped. She shook her head. "This is gooier than I thought!" She held out a little caramel for the bird Cara was cleaning. "Sweet thing," she cooed.

Cara rinsed the bird's feathers again. "This one is going to be okay," she said. "But there are so many others. I'm not sure we'll be able to wash them all."

"That's why *we're* here to help!" Berry said, landing next to Cara.

"We got the sugar fly message," Dash told Melli.

"And we came as fast as we could," Raina added.

Melli was touched that all her friends had gotten to Caramel Hills so quickly. She smiled at the Fruit Fairy, Mint Fairy, and Gummy Fairy standing before her.

The fairies immediately started to care for the butterscotch-coated birds. As they worked Melli kept looking around. The flow of syrup was steady, and the spill was growing larger.

"Raina, why do you think this happened?" Melli asked.

Raina usually had the answers to questions.

She loved to read and was known to have memorized many sections of the Fairy Code Book. The thick volume of the history of Sugar Valley had helped the friends solve mysteries around Candy Kingdom in the past.

"Butterscotch Volcano is dormant," Raina said. "That means it doesn't erupt for long periods of time." She paused and glanced at her friends. "This doesn't mean that it *couldn't* erupt."

"And we know there is butterscotch in there because the fairies filled barrels at the Butterscotch Festival," Dash added.

"Dash is right," Melli agreed. "But it took a week to fill all the barrels at the castle." She glanced over at the volcano. "No, this is very different. I want to go take a closer look. Anyone want to come?"

"I will," Cocoa called. "I've never seen so much butterscotch syrup!"

"We're *all* going with you," Berry said.

Raina and Dash lined up next to the Fruit Fairy. They had finished cleaning a bird and were worried about the amount of syrup too.

All five fairies flew up in the air. Melli took a fast dive near the volcano. Her friends followed.

"Look!" Melli shouted. "There's the crack on the side of the volcano! The older Caramel Fairies were right. It's enormous!"

"No wonder there is an overrun of syrup," Cocoa said.

"A leaky volcano?" Dash asked, wrinkling her nose.

They all looked to Raina. She shrugged. "It can happen," she said. She peered down at the volcano. "Maybe there was an eruption that made the volcano crack?" She tapped her finger to her chin. "That seems the most likely answer."

"Hot caramel," Melli muttered.

"You mean hot butterscotch," Dash said, correcting her.

"This isn't good news at all," Cocoa said.

"No, it's not," Melli replied. She looked at her friends. "The question is, how do we stop this butterscotch burst?"

CHAPTER 3

Big Burst

The fairies huddled together on a branch of a caramel tree. From where they were sitting, they could see the butterscotch spreading.

"We have to do something–and fast," Melli said.

"Those poor birds," Raina whispered as she looked below. "The butterscotch in their wings

will keep them from flying. They'll never be able to get food."

Melli felt helpless. Usually she adored Butterscotch Volcano and the rich syrup that was inside. Making candies with the fresh, hot butterscotch was always a highlight of the Butterscotch Festival. Melli loved watching the brave Caramel Fairies dip into the center of the volcano to scoop out the sweet, golden treat. She had never imagined how dangerous the volcano could be!

"The butterscotch is out of control," she said sadly.

Dash flew off the branch and quickly circled the area. When she came back to the branch, she had a sour look on her face. "If we don't stop the leak, the butterscotch will reach Chocolate

Woods. Think of all the animals there—and the chocolate crops!"

"Double-dip bittersweet," Cocoa said, hanging her head.

"We need to stop this," Berry said, sitting down next to Melli.

"Maybe we should be asking *whom* to stop?" Melli asked.

"Mogu?" Cocoa asked. She wrinkled her nose. "Do you think that salty old troll could have done this?"

Melli shivered. The thought of Mogu in Caramel Hills upset her. The greedy troll often tried to steal Candy Fairy candy, but he usually stayed under his bridge in Black Licorice Swamp. She looked to her friends.

"I'm not sure if this is his style," Berry said,

thinking aloud. "The butterscotch from the volcano is yummy, but it's not in candy form. You'd have to do a lot of work to make candy, or have the patience to wait for the butterscotch to cool."

"Doing work and having patience don't seem like Mogu's style," Raina said, agreeing with Berry.

Cocoa fluttered her wings and looked around. "But if Mogu is greedy enough, he might."

"No, Mogu wouldn't be patient enough," Melli said with certainty. "Having patience is one of the hardest parts of being a Caramel Fairy."

"Which is why I like to work with mint," Dash said, grinning. She reached into her pocket and took out a peppermint. "Ahh," she said. "Quick and tasty!"

Melli smiled at her minty friend. No one liked speed better than her friend Dash. She was one of the smallest Candy Fairies, and also one of the fastest. *And* the least patient fairy she knew!

"The more I think about it, I think it's possible the crack just happened naturally," Raina suggested. She slipped the Fairy Code Book out of her bag. "Yes, I have the book," she said to her friends before they could comment. Usually one of her friends couldn't help making fun of her for always having the fact book on hand. In the past the thick volume of the history of Sugar Valley had helped the friends solve mysteries that happened in Candy Kingdom.

"Let's hope there's something in the book that can help us figure out this sticky mess," Melli said.

As the fairies hovered over the book Melli heard her sister call to her.

"Let me go check on Cara," she said to her friends. "I'll be right back."

Down at the bottom of the tree, birds surrounded Cara.

"Melli," Cara gasped when she saw her big sister. "There are so many sticky caramellas! Two Caramel Fairies just left more here for us to clean." Cara's brown eyes were full of tears. "How will we ever save them all?"

Melli hugged her sister. Seeing her so upset made Melli stronger. "We will help one bird at a time," she said. "If we work together, we can figure this out." She pointed up at the tree behind them. "Raina is looking up some facts in the Fairy Code Book. She's sure to find some useful information."

"I hope so," Cara said. "In the meantime, this area will be the rescue center. I'm going to get some more supplies. Can you stay here? I think more caramellas will be coming."

"Sure as sugar, I'll stay," Melli said. She watched her sister fly off, and then she picked up a sticky bird. She carefully wiped its wings and tried to get the syrup off.

Suddenly the sounds of gurgling and rumbling filled the air. It sounded as if a giant was awaking from his slumber. Melli froze. She looked toward the volcano. The crack she had spotted earlier was now split open wider. More butterscotch rolled up to Melli's feet. The spill was getting deeper and deeper . . . and more dangerous for everyone in Caramel Hills.

Cara came up behind her. "Oh no," she

moaned. "More butterscotch! What are we going to do?"

"I'm going to see if the other fairies have come up with a plan," Melli said. "Will you be all right?"

"Yes," Cara said bravely. "I'll work on cleaning the birds. You work on stopping this spill!"

Melli smiled at her little sister. "I'm so proud of you," she said. "I'll try to be back soon."

Soon, she thought, *before this mess gets bigger.*

CHAPTER 4

Chocolate Aid

Melli rushed back to the caramel tree where her friends huddled together. Raina was in the middle of the group with the Fairy Code Book on her lap. Melli hoped that while she had been with Cara the fairies had thought of a plan. This latest burst of butterscotch from the volcano had created even more trouble.

"We're in a hot butterscotch emergency," Melli cried as she flew up to the tree. "Now the spill is even deeper than before!"

"Take a breath," Cocoa told Melli. "We can't panic. We need to focus." She held out her hand to Melli. "Come sit down for a minute." She moved over to make room on the branch for her friend.

Melli knew Cocoa was right, but seeing more butterscotch flow from the volcano was upsetting. "It's getting worse down there," she said sadly.

"More butterscotch?" Dash asked. Her blue eyes were wide and full of fear.

"But we found something in the Fairy Code Book that might work," Raina said, giving Dash a stern look. "Remember, we have to remain calm." She held up the book to show Melli the picture. "We could build a barricade to block the butterscotch from spilling out into Chocolate Woods," Raina said slowly. "The idea is from this story about an overflow from Chocolate River."

"A barricade?" Melli said as she studied the picture.

"You see, Chocolate Fairies used bark and branches from a chocolate oak tree and tied them together, " Cocoa explained. "The bundle blocked the flow of chocolate coming from the rising river."

"The barricade saved Chocolate Woods," Berry added.

Melli bit her nails and looked up at her friends. "But butterscotch is much thicker and stickier than chocolate from Chocolate River. Will a chocolate barricade really work?"

Cocoa put her arm around Melli. "Chocolate Woods is so close. Let's get some chocolate branches and bark and give it a try."

"Chocolate is not the strongest material. It tends to flake," Dash pointed out.

Cocoa scowled at Dash. "We should at least try."

Melli turned to Dash. Everyone was feeling the pressure of the situation, and Melli didn't want her friends to fight. But Dash was a master at building sleds. She was one of the fastest racers in Sugar Valley and had even made her own sled and won a medal at the Marshmallow Run sled race. "Dash, do you have another suggestion?" Melli asked.

Dash looked down at the ground. "I don't know what would hold the syrup back," she said quietly. "Especially hot butterscotch."

The friends all glanced down at the spill.

"Cocoa is right," Melli said, breaking the silence. "Chocolate Woods is nearby and the easiest place for us to get materials. At least we can try to keep the spill from spreading so fast."

The fairies nodded in agreement. They flew off to the woods and gathered pieces of bark, twigs, and branches from the chocolate oaks. They put the materials on a large blanket, and each fairy took a corner. Melli flew in front to lead the way.

For the first time since she had seen the spill, Melli had a feeling of hope. Now if only this chocolate barricade would solve the problem!

Near the base of the volcano the five friends put the chocolate logs and bark on the ground. When the last of the wood was unloaded, Melli stood back and held her breath.

"Look!" she cried out. "The barricade is working!"

Butterscotch wasn't passing through the chocolate barricade. The five fairies joined hands and did a little dance. But their rejoicing didn't last long. After a few moments their feet were covered in the thick golden syrup.

Cocoa hung her head. "You were right, Dash," she said. "I'm sorry."

"We had to try," Dash said. "I'm really sorry that this didn't work. The chocolate wasn't strong or sticky enough to hold back the butterscotch."

Melli's wings fluttered and a smile appeared on her face. "Dash! That's it!" she exclaimed. Her feet lifted off the ground as she fluttered her wings. "That's the answer!" she shouted. Her friends stared at her, amazed at her outburst. "We need something that will be sticky and sturdy for sealing the crack," she said.

Raina, Cocoa, Dash, and Berry waited for Melli to explain.

"Bubble gum!" Melli finally exclaimed. She saw that her friends still didn't understand her idea. "If we can get enough sticky bubble gum, first we'll seal this crack, and then we'll be able to plug it up and stop the butterscotch from leaking!"

Raina considered Melli's plan. "I think you're on to something. Bubble gum would be an excellent choice. It's strong and sticky, and it would fill up the crack. But we'll need a lot of it."

"My cousin Pinkie makes bubble gum," Melli said enthusiastically. "She can help! She works at Candy Castle."

"Well then, let's go see her now!" Berry said.

Melli quickly wrote a sugar fly message to Cara explaining that she would be back shortly—with another plan. Melli hoped this time their idea would work. Already there were too many birds harmed by the butterscotch spill.

"Let's hope this is a pink solution that will stick!" Melli said as she took the lead and flew toward Candy Castle.

CHAPTER
5

Think Big

When the five fairies arrived at Candy Castle, there was a large group of fairies gathered in the Royal Gardens. The guards had just sounded their caramel horns, and Princess Lolli was standing on her balcony. The kind and gentle ruler was trying to quiet the crowd just as the fairies landed in the garden.

"Look!" Melli said. "We're just in time for Princess Lolli's announcement."

"Unfortunately, we've seen firsthand what is going on in Caramel Hills," Raina said. "I'm sure that is what she is going to talk about."

"Shh," Berry scolded. "She's ready to speak."

"Good afternoon," Princess Lolli said to the fairies in the Royal Gardens. "I know many of you have heard about the trouble in Caramel Hills. It is a very sad day." The princess looked around at the crowd. "There is a large crack near the base of the volcano, and hot butterscotch is leaking out into the hills."

Heavy sighs were heard throughout the crowd.

If only they could all see what is happening there now, Melli thought sadly.

"The caramella birds that live up in the hills are in the greatest danger," Princess Lolli continued. "We need to work together to stop the spill and clean the animals that have been covered in the hot butterscotch."

"The news certainly has traveled fast," Cocoa said, looking around the Royal Gardens.

"We'll need everyone's help in the kingdom," Melli said. "I'm so glad to see so many fairies here."

"Sugar Valley is under a Kingdom Emergency," Princess Lolli declared. "All fairies are expected to help out in Caramel Hills. I hope to have more news for you soon." The princess turned to her right and waved her hand. Tula, one of Princess Lolli's advisers, appeared. "Tula will head the cleanup project. Please see her so we can get started as soon as possible."

The princess bowed her head and stepped back into the castle. Everyone felt her sadness. Princess Lolli was a good friend to all the creatures in Sugar Valley. Melli knew that this news was weighing heavily on her heart.

"Come," Melli said to her friends. "Let's go talk to Princess Lolli. I want to tell her about my plan."

The fairies flew into the castle. They waited patiently while the palace guard asked permission for them to enter the throne room. They found Princess Lolli near the window, looking out toward Caramel Hills.

"Princess Lolli, Caramel Hills is so awful," Melli blurted out. She ran up to the princess. "The caramella birds are trapped in the thick, hot butterscotch."

Princess Lolli gave Melli a tight hug. "I know," she said. "This is very disturbing news."

"But, Princess Lolli, we have a plan," Melli said, brightening. "A plan we think will work."

"At first we thought that if we could barricade the butterscotch, we could stop the leak, but that didn't work," Cocoa confessed. "The chocolate wood wasn't strong enough to hold the hot syrup."

"So instead, we thought we could seal the crack," Melli added.

Princess Lolli turned to face the five fairies before her. Her eyebrows shot up. "Tell me more," she said.

"My cousin Pinkie makes bubble gum here at the castle," Melli said. "If we can help her make enough sticky bubble gum, we might be able to mend the side of the volcano."

Princess Lolli smiled. "That is a fantastic idea," she said. "I am so impressed, and I'm grateful for your creative thinking." She walked over to her throne and sat down. "I think that is certainly worth a try!"

Melli was ready to burst with pride.

"Have you spoken to Pinkie?" Princess Lolli asked.

Melli shook her head. "We wanted to see what you thought about the idea first," she said.

Princess Lolli looked back out the window toward Caramel Hills. "Let's hope Pinkie can make enough gum."

"We'll help her," Melli offered.

"Thank you," Princess Lolli said. She called for one of the guards. "Please find Pinkie and ask her to come to the throne room at once." Then she faced Melli. "I must go speak to Tula before she leaves for Caramel Hills. You and your friends wait here for Pinkie. I'll be back shortly."

Melli and her friends looked at one another in amazement. They had been in Princess Lolli's throne room before, but they had never been there alone. They stood very still, not sure what to do.

Suddenly Melli began pacing around the room. "I hope Pinkie gets here soon."

"She'll be here," Cocoa told her. "Don't worry."

A short while later Pinkie flew into the throne room. She hugged Melli and her friends. She had heard about the Butterscotch Volcano disaster but had not realized how serious it had become. When Melli filled her in, her eyes started to brim with tears.

"And so we need to stop the leak in the

volcano," Melli said. "We thought your bubble gum could be the plug."

Pinkie tilted her head and flapped her pale pink wings. "I'm not sure I can do that," she said.

This was not the reply Melli had expected to hear. Her wings drooped down to the floor.

"I only make tiny pieces of bubble gum, Melli," Pinkie said. She dipped her hand into her pocket and pulled out three minia-ture gumballs.

Melli glanced up at her friends. Then her eyes settled on Princess Lolli's throne. The tall, wide peppermint sticks that Dash had created for the princess made the throne extra-special.

Melli thought back to when Dash had been growing the peppermint sticks for the princess's new throne and training for the Marshmallow Run. No one had believed that Dash could both manage her training and create the large royal peppermints, but she had. Melli moved closer to Dash.

"When you were making the peppermint sticks for the throne, they were the biggest sticks you had ever made, right?" Melli asked.

Dash nodded. She reached into her bag for a snack.

"Did you do anything differently?" Melli asked.

Taking a nibble of her treat, Dash shook her head. "Not really," she said.

"They took longer to grow, but those sticks are the same as the small ones right here." Dash showed off a smaller peppermint stick in her hand.

"And I bet those taste the same," Cocoa said, smiling. She winked at Melli. She knew exactly what her clever friend was doing.

"Sure as sugar!" Dash exclaimed.

"You see, Pinkie," Melli said, jumping up, "it's still the same bubble gum. You just have to make much, much, much more."

"We can help you create the most bubble gum ever," Raina said. "You can do this, Pinkie!"

"We're all counting on you," Melli told her.

Pinkie looked concerned, but Melli hoped Dash's peppermint sticks would inspire her cousin—and change her mind.

CHAPTER

6

A Sugar-tastic Idea

Melli's wings twitched as she waited to hear Pinkie's reply. She hoped her cousin would agree to make a superbig bubble gum plug for the volcano. Waiting for her to answer was so hard! She crossed her fingers. Then she listened to her four friends, who surrounded Pinkie.

"We're asking for your help for all the cara-mella birds in Caramel Hills," Cocoa said.

Melli shot her friend Cocoa a grateful look.

"Maybe if you went to Caramel Hills and saw the problem close-up, you'd understand why we desperately need your help," Raina said. "You could see what your bubble gum will do."

Melli was thankful for Raina's calm and thoughtful response. And it seemed to help Pinkie with her decision.

The small Bubble Gum Fairy fluttered her wings. She raised her eyebrows and let out a deep breath. "Will you all come with me?" she asked.

"Sure as sugar!" the five friends said in unison.

The fairies flew out of Candy Castle and

across the kingdom to Caramel Hills. As they flew along Chocolate River, Melli glanced over at Pinkie.

"I know this seems crazy to you," Melli said. "But I really think bubble gum is the answer."

Pinkie nodded. "I need to see the problem before I try to make a solution," she said.

Melli understood. She hoped that when Pinkie saw the cracked volcano, she'd realize why bubble gum was their best shot at fixing the leak. She led Pinkie and her friends straight to Butterscotch Volcano. At the bottom of the volcano Melli spotted Cara and flew down to greet her.

"I'm so glad you're back," Cara blurted out. "The butterscotch is spreading fast—and heading dangerously close to Chocolate Woods."

"It would be a disastrous and delicious mess in Chocolate Woods," Dash said with a wistful look in her eyes.

Melli knew that Dash often thought with her stomach first. She smiled at her, knowing that she meant no harm.

"We brought Pinkie here because we're hoping she can make a bubble gum seal for the leak in the volcano," Melli told her. She turned around and saw Pinkie with her mouth gaping open.

"This is awful," Pinkie said softly. "Show me the crack."

Taking her hand, Melli and Pinkie left the butterscotch-covered ground and flew up to the side of the volcano to take a closer look at the leak.

"Here it is," Melli said, pointing. "You can see how the butterscotch is pooling on the flat land."

Pinkie stared at the volcano for a minute. "Wow, that's a mighty big crack."

"Do you think you can make enough bubble gum for us, Pinkie?" Melli asked. She knew seeing the sticky situation firsthand had made her want to help.

"I am going to try my hardest," Pinkie told her. "I'll need more time and some extra Candy Fairy help."

"Take Berry and Raina with you," Melli said. "They will be excellent helpers. Dash, Cocoa, and I will stay here with Cara."

"That sounds like a perfect pink plan," Pinkie said. "Let's meet back here before Sun Dip."

Melli hugged Pinkie. "Thank you," she said.

"I'll see you later." Then she smiled at her cousin. "Good luck!"

While Berry, Raina, and Pinkie returned to Candy Castle, Cocoa, Dash, and Melli went to see how they could help Cara.

"Tula just dropped off more supplies," Cara said. She pointed to a few boxes lying on the ground.

"I can unpack and organize those things," Cocoa offered.

"I'll start cleaning these little birds over here, okay, Cara?" Melli asked.

"They've been waiting a long time," Cara said. "They'll be glad to be butterscotch-free."

For the next few hours the fairies worked hard washing caramella birds of every shape and size. When the birds were free of butterscotch,

they swooped through the air, happy to fly once again.

"I've cleaned so many birds, but there are still more who are covered in this goo," Melli told her friends.

"It's a butterscotch disaster, all right," Dash sighed. Then she bent down to dip her finger in the thick butterscotch pool. "But I have to admit, this syrup is *really* delicious," she said, licking her finger.

"Leave it to Dash to still have an appetite even during a full-on Candy Kingdom emergency," Cocoa said. She crossed her arms across her chest.

For the first time since Melli had spotted the first butterscotch-coated bird, she laughed.

Dash's stomach was reliable—she was hungry all the time!

"I'm serious," Dash said, blushing.

Cocoa started to laugh. "I know you are," she said, smiling. "Believe me, I wish I could use all this good butterscotch. What a waste."

Melli's face lit up. "Hot caramel!" she screamed.

Dash and Cocoa looked at her. "What happened?" they said at the same time.

Fluttering her wings excitedly, Melli flew up in the air. "Nothing happened," she explained. "Except that you both gave me a *sugar-tastic* idea!" When she saw that her friends still looked confused, she said, "The butterscotch is delicious, and it is a shame that fairies can't use the syrup. This is an awful waste."

"Why is she saying what we already know?" Dash whispered to Cocoa.

"Because you're right!" Melli exclaimed. "We need to store and save the butterscotch. Let's get those big barrels from Candy Castle here and fill them with butterscotch."

"*Sweeeeet!*" Dash cheered.

"Maybe that would lower the level of the syrup pool here too," Cocoa said. "Look how high the butterscotch is now."

Dash held up her hand. "Wait a minty minute. *How* are we going to get the syrup into the barrels? And how are we going to get the barrels from the castle here to Caramel Hills?"

Melli sighed. "I didn't think of that. Any ideas?"

"Where's Raina with her Fairy Code Book when you need her?" Cocoa said with a sigh.

Melli thought back to the last Butterscotch Festival. She remembered there were tubes set up from the volcano that led to the caramel barrels. "We need tubes," she said. "Something to pour the syrup in and move it from one place to another." She turned to Dash. "What would you make a tube out of?"

Dash thought for a moment. She snapped her fingers. "Toffee," she called out. "It's strong and slippery. I think toffee candy will be perfect."

Melli gave Dash a hug. "Sure as sugar, this is going to work! Dash, you get the toffee, and Cocoa and I will get the barrels."

"*So mint!*" Dash said. "I know just the toffee tree to visit for a good strong piece. It might take me a while to carve out a tube, but I'll try."

"Dash," Melli said, "I'm sure you'll do a

sugar-tastic job! We'll meet you back here before Sun Dip."

Feeling a burst of energy, Melli and Cocoa flew back to Candy Castle. Melli knew they'd find a large barrel there for them to take back to hold the butterscotch. Now all the syrup would not go to waste. And maybe, just maybe, they could stop the spill from spreading all over Sugar Valley.

CHAPTER 7

Supersweet

At Candy Castle there were fairies flying busily around. With the kingdom in a state of emergency, everyone in Sugar Valley was helping out. So many fairies cared about Caramel Hills.

"There's Tula," Melli said. "Cocoa, let's ask her about finding some empty barrels. I'm sure she can help us."

The two fairies flew over to Tula, who was surrounded by a large group of fairies. She had a scroll and a long feather pen in her hands.

"Lemona, please take your crew of Sour Orchard Fairies to the animal rescue center set up in Caramel Hills," Tula said. "You'll find Cara the Caramel Fairy there, and she will advise you."

Melli's heart swelled with pride. She wanted to shout, "That's my little sister!" She watched as the group of Sour Orchard Fairies flew off. Berry was friends with Lemona. One time Berry had even gone to Sour Orchard, and Lemona had been very nice to her. Once again Melli was touched that so many fairies wanted to help.

"We're next," Cocoa said, pulling Melli closer to Tula.

Tula didn't even look up from her scroll. Melli wasn't sure if she should speak first. She looked over at Cocoa, who nodded toward Tula.

"Go ahead," Cocoa urged her friend. "Tell her your plan."

Melli cleared her throat. She suddenly felt as if her voice would not come out. She took a deep breath. "Tula," she said, "we have an idea about storing the overflow of butterscotch from the volcano."

Tula peered over her sugarcoated glasses at the two young fairies in front of her.

Cocoa squeezed Melli's hand, encouraging her to go on.

"You see, the extra butterscotch is causing so much trouble," Melli said quickly. "If we can get some of the syrup into barrels like we did at the

Butterscotch Festival, we could stop the overflow and save the butterscotch syrup for later." Melli waited as Tula turned her gaze on her.

"Your name is Melli, right?" Tula said, staring at her.

"Yes," Melli said quietly. She stood perfectly still. She hoped that Tula thought she had a good idea.

"Melli," Tula said. She took off her glasses and looked into Melli's eyes. "Not one other fairy here has come up with such a good suggestion."

Melli looked down at her feet and fluttered her wings.

"Princess Lolli is not here," Tula went on. "She is at Butterscotch Volcano. But I think that is a supersweet idea. I like when a fairy is thinking! We'll have to get some of the palace guards to carry the large barrels over to Caramel Hills. Will you fly with them and direct the project?"

"Sure as sugar!" Melli replied. "I would be happy to show them where to go."

"Let me speak to the guards, and you can meet them out by the Royal Gardens," Tula said. "Give me about ten minutes."

"Thank you!" Melli said, bursting with pride.

Cocoa pulled Melli's hand. "While we're waiting, let's see how Pinkie is doing," she said.

Melli and Cocoa flew over to the bubble gum garden, just outside the Royal Gardens gate. In the middle of the garden Melli saw Berry, Raina, and Pinkie standing over a wide barrel.

"How is everything going?" Melli asked as she landed next to Pinkie. She looked into the bowl and saw a mound of pink gum.

Pinkie pulled the long paddle out of the barrel. Stretching her arm up high, she showed off the fresh batch of bubble gum. "Berry and Raina have helped me so much," she said. "With their encouragement and their sweet ways, I think we've made the largest wad of bubble gum ever!"

The pink sticky candy looked good enough to eat—and sticky enough to plug up a crack. "I think you're right!" Melli exclaimed. She clapped her hands together.

Cocoa filled them in on the plan with the barrels and Dash's project of building a tube for the butterscotch syrup.

"Good thinking," Raina said.

Melli blushed. "I remembered a chapter in the Fairy Code Book about the Butterscotch Festival," she said.

Raina's eyes sparkled. "Ah, you did!" she said. "Lickin' lollipops!"

"We need to make some more bubble gum," Pinkie told her cousin. "That volcano crack was very wide and deep. We should probably make another batch this size."

Melli agreed. "We still have a little more time before Sun Dip," she said. "Cocoa and I are going to fly back to Caramel Hills with the barrels. Will you meet us there?"

"Yes," Pinkie said. "Before Sun Dip for sure— just as we planned."

"You'll need some guards to fly this gum over to Caramel Hills," Melli told her friends. "There's no way you'll be able to pick up this barrel!"

Raina laughed. "We already spoke to Tula

about getting guards to help us," she said. "Don't worry. We'll see you later."

Melli and Cocoa and four palace guards flew back to the volcano with four large barrels. The barrels might not hold all the overflowing butterscotch, but it was a start. And that was the best she could hope for right now.

8

A Sticky Plan

Back at Caramel Hills there was a swarm of fairies flying near the volcano. Melli's heart started to pound.

"Maybe something awful has happened while we were at Candy Castle," she said to Cocoa. She tried to see the volcano, but there were too many fairies in the way. "I can't see a thing!" she cried. "Do you think the volcano erupted? Oh, that would be awful! Then there'd be even more butterscotch flowing over Caramel Hills."

Cocoa shook her head. "Just calm down," she said. "If Berry were here, she'd tell you not to dip your wings in syrup yet." Flapping her wings, Cocoa leaped higher in the air and squinted her eyes.

"Do you see anything?" Melli called up to her. She couldn't bear the thought of more syrup rushing over the hills.

"Nothing happened, I think!" Cocoa shouted. "Come up here. I see Princess Lolli." She pointed to the center of the crowd. "There are a bunch of castle guards surrounding her. She must be here to see the volcano firsthand."

Melli flew up next to Cocoa. It was easy to

spot Princess Lolli's strawberry-blond hair and her sugarcoated sparkly tiara. She was examining the crack and the damage done by the hot, sticky syrup.

"I want to tell her about our plan with the barrels," Melli said. "I'm sure she'll be pleased." She darted quickly in and out of the crowd to where Princess Lolli was talking to one of her advisers.

"Princess Lolli," Melli called. She waved and flew close to her.

"Hello, Melli," Princess Lolli said. "How is Pinkie coming along with the bubble gum? We will need a very big wad of gum to plug this crack."

"She's working on it," Melli informed her. "Berry and Raina are helping out." She took a deep breath. She was so anxious to tell Princess Lolli her idea about saving some of the overflowing butterscotch that she was having trouble breathing!

Princess Lolli put a hand on her back. "What is it, Melli?" she said kindly. "Is there something more?"

"Yes," Melli said. "Cocoa and I have another idea that might save the butterscotch and stop some of the overflow. We spoke to Tula about the plan. Would you like to hear it?"

Princess Lolli's eyes widened. "I'd love to hear some good news, or at least a good idea right about now," she said.

Melli explained the plan while Cocoa showed

the castle guards where to put the barrels.

"We thought if we could capture some of the butterscotch, the spill wouldn't get wider," Melli told the princess.

Princess Lolli's wings fluttered. "This is a fine idea," she said, "but how will we get the butterscotch into the barrels?"

Dash flew up behind the princess and Melli with a long, narrow toffee tube in her arms. "With this!" she cried. "We can stick it in the crack and seal the gum around the tube. Then all the butterscotch will flow through it and into the barrel."

Princess Lolli examined the tube. A smile spread across her face. "Sure as sugar, it's worth a try!" she declared.

"The bubble gum should be ready before Sun

Dip," Melli said. She looked up to the sky. It would be a little longer before the sun touched the tips of the Frosted Mountains.

"We'll have to be patient," Princess Lolli said, seeing disappointment in Melli's face. "I'm going to check in with the rescue center. Keep an eye out for Pinkie and the others. Send for me when they arrive so we can all be a part of Bubble Gum Rescue."

Melli watched Princess Lolli as she flew away from the volcano and back down to the animal rescue center. Normally, the princess had a lovely smile on her face. But today, Melli noticed, there was a deep crease in her forehead and she looked very troubled. She knew that seeing all the animals in danger broke the princess's heart.

"We need the bubble gum now," Melli said.

"Don't worry," Cocoa said. She was back from helping the guards with the barrels. "Pinkie will come. For now we should go help at the animal rescue center, don't you think?"

Melli followed Cocoa down to the base of the volcano and joined the other fairies. Working together made the task go faster, and time moved quickly.

After Melli finished washing her fifth cara-mella bird, she glanced up at the sky. The sun was nearing the tip of the Frosted Mountains.

Where is Pinkie? She has to get here! Melli thought.

Cocoa could see that her friend was worry-ing more and more. "Let's go back up to the volcano," Cocoa said to Melli. "They should be back soon."

Together, the two fairies hovered in the sky,

and just then Melli saw Berry, Raina, Dash, and Pinkie flying toward the volcano. Behind them were four palace guards holding the two large barrels of pink bubble gum.

"We've got bubble gum!" Berry announced as she drew closer. "Bubble Gum Rescue is ready to begin!"

"That is sweet news to hear on this dreadfully gooey day," Melli called. She flew up to Pinkie and gave her a hug. "I knew you could do this!" she cried.

"Pinkie whipped up the biggest and the stickiest bubble gum batch ever," Raina added.

"And I wouldn't have been able to do it without Berry and Raina's help," Pinkie told her cousin.

"Cocoa, go get Princess Lolli," Melli said. "Tell her we're ready to start the rescue!"

"I'll be back in a flash," Cocoa said, speeding down to the bottom of the volcano.

"Pinkie, all this bubble gum is fantastic!" Melli said. She peered into the barrel. "This just has to work!" she cried.

"I hope so," Pinkie said. She couldn't take her eyes off the large crack in the side of the mountain.

"Bubble Gum Rescue will work," Melli said. "You'll see."

She crossed her fingers and hoped that her prediction would come true.

9

Pink and Positive

Melli and her friends hovered near the crack on the side of Butterscotch Volcano, waiting for Cocoa to return with Princess Lolli. *Oh, please hurry,* Melli thought as she kept watch for Cocoa and the fairy princess.

"What happens if there isn't enough bubble gum?" Pinkie asked as she hovered beside Melli.

"That crack is so deep. I'm not sure we've made enough to patch it up." Pinkie's pale pink wings were beating quickly, and her forehead was wrinkled with worry.

Melli was concerned too. She looked over at Berry and Raina, who were bobbing up and down in the wind. If only she could be as calm as her friends!

"Don't worry, Pinkie," Melli managed to say. "Whatever you made will help. Let's try to think positive."

Pinkie nodded. "I'll try," she said. "Pink and positive," she muttered over and over.

When Melli spotted Cocoa and Princess Lolli, she waved both her arms in the air and called out to them. "Over here! Oh, sweet sugar, they're finally here."

Cocoa waved back, and the two fairies flew toward them.

"Hello," Princess Lolli said, greeting the fairies. "Cocoa said that the bubble gum is ready. This is certainly sweet news."

"Yes," Pinkie said. "But we need help. The barrels of bubble gum are too heavy. We can't lift them."

"The guards are here to assist you," Princess Lolli said. She flew over and peered into one of the containers. "This is very fine work," she called. "Thank you." She smiled at Pinkie, Berry, and Raina.

"Let Bubble Gum Rescue begin!" Princess Lolli declared.

Then she turned to one of the castle guards. "Let's spread the gum around and see if we can seal the crack."

In a flash the guards moved the barrels closer to the volcano.

Dash took the long toffee tube she had cradled in her arms up to the crack. "I hope this works," she said. "We'll all need to hold the tube in place while the guards pour the bubble gum."

Melli saw Pinkie's confused expression, so she explained Dash's plan.

"We have some yummy ideas for all that butterscotch," Dash whispered to Pinkie.

Princess Lolli regarded the toffee tube. "This is *so mint*, Dash," she said with a smile.

Melli glanced over at Dash. She saw her minty friend blushing to the shade of red in a candy cane. "Thank you," she said.

"Oh, peppermint sticks!" Dash exclaimed. "It was the least I could do. I couldn't stand to see all that butterscotch wasted." She leaned in closer to Melli. "Promise me a special butter-scotch candy later?"

Laughing, Melli hugged Dash. "Bubbling butterscotch, you've got yourself a deal!" she cried.

The Candy Castle guards poured the bubble gum from the barrels. With long, heavy paddles, they spread the sticky mixture into the crack.

Melli and her friends grabbed one end of the tube, holding it in the crack as the guards filled bubble gum in around it.

"All right," one of the guards called. "You can let go. The tube is secure."

The five fairies held their breath and flew up in the air.

"I don't know if I can look," said Cocoa.

"Yes, you can! Open your eyes, Cocoa. It's a sweet surprise!" said Melli.

No more butterscotch was leaking out of the volcano's side! Instead, a steady stream of the golden syrup was pouring out of the tube—and into a large barrel off to the side.

"Hot butterscotch!" Melli cheered.

"We did it!" Cocoa shouted.

A roar of applause rose up in Caramel Hills. All the fairies rejoiced and sang out. Bubble Gum Rescue was a huge success!

Melli rushed over to Pinkie. "Thank you," she said. "I knew you could do this."

Pinkie squeezed her cousin tight. "I never would have thought of this idea. Thank you for dreaming it up." She turned to face Berry and Raina. "And thank you, too!"

"We were happy to lend some sugar," Raina said, grinning.

"Sweet strawberries," Berry said, coming up to Pinkie. "You did all the work, Pinkie. You should be extra-proud."

This was a time to celebrate, but Melli couldn't stop thinking of the caramella birds at the base of the volcano. There were still many suffering because of the butterscotch spill.

"What's wrong, Melli?" Cocoa asked. "You don't look happy. You should be! We just stopped the gushing butterscotch—and even managed to save the syrup."

Melli looked down at her feet. "I know," she said softly. She couldn't even speak about the awful thought that had popped into her head. "But . . ." She couldn't get the words out.

Raina flew up next to her. "Are you worried about the caramella birds?" she asked. "Why don't we check in on the rescue center now?"

Melli hoped the animals in the center would be all right—especially if all the Candy Fairies continued to help. But that was not the only thing bothering her.

"Tell us," Cocoa said. "Please."

Melli bit her nails. "It's just . . ." She knew she had to say the words quickly, otherwise she wouldn't be able to tell her friends. Melli took a deep breath. She started to explain. "Now the crack is sealed and the gushing butterscotch syrup stopped." She paused and looked at the concerned faces surrounding her. "But what if this happens again?" Melli asked, her voice trembling. She watched her friends' expressions.

Each Candy Fairy had the same sad look. They were thinking the same sour thought.

None of them could have predicted what had happened in Caramel Hills. And they wouldn't be able to prevent the volcano from cracking or erupting.

Melli looked to each of her friends. But she knew that none of them had a magic answer for her.

CHAPTER
10

Bubbles of Happiness

Melli's question hung in the air. None of the fairies knew how to respond. Luckily, Princess Lolli was close enough to hear the question, and she immediately flew to the fairies.

"Melli, you asked a very good question," Princess Lolli told her. "There are many events we can be prepared for in Sugar Valley. We can try to prevent sour things from happening, but there is much we can't predict or prevent." She motioned for the fairies to move closer. When the fairies were huddled together, she continued. "Sadly, many events that happen are out of our control."

"Like a volcano leaking," Melli said.

"Or a river overflowing," Cocoa added.

"Even a rainstorm," Raina said softly.

"Yes, there are many things that happen naturally here in the valley," Princess Lolli said. "But working together can make life sweeter and safer. All the fairies in the kingdom should feel very proud for lending a helping hand."

Raina took the Fairy Code Book from her bag and showed the first page. "That's what the Fairy Code Book says too." She read, "'Nature can't

always be predicted, so take care and be aware.'"

Princess Lolli nodded. "We all need to watch out for one another . . . and keep an eye out for leaking volcanoes!"

All of a sudden Cara came racing up to the group. "Please, come quick!" she cried.

"What's happened?" Melli asked. Cara looked upset, and Melli worried one of the cara-mella birds might be seriously injured.

"Please," Cara begged. "Come now!"

The fairies raced quickly to the animal rescue center. Melli could hardly breathe she was so nervous.

But once there Melli found quite a sight. Instead of finding a seriously wounded caramella, she saw a group of birds happy and clean.

"The caramella birds want to thank you all for your clever work," Cara said proudly. "I was bursting to tell you, but I promised that I would make this a surprise."

Melli hugged her little sister. "You've been pure as sugar," she said. "Thank you for helping so much with the rescue center."

"This is the sweetest part of the day," Cara said, hugging her sister. "I'm so glad that Caramel Hills is almost back to normal.

"With extra butterscotch!" Dash blurted out.

She looked around at the barrels of butterscotch that had already been filled. "It's like the Butterscotch Festival has come early this year."

"Dash, that is an excellent idea," Princess Lolli said, smiling. "Why not have a celebration now? All the fairies worked so hard to rescue the caramellas and save Caramel Hills. I think we should have a party!"

"A bubblicious party!" Pinkie exclaimed.

"I couldn't think of anything more fitting for this occasion," the princess proclaimed.

With a declaration from Princess Lolli, the fairies started to fly . . . and soon the rescue center had been turned into a place fit for a royal celebration.

Pinkie, Berry, and Raina were a *sugar-ific* team again and created delicious bubble gum bubbles.

"A rainbow of bubbles," Melli said when she saw the colorful decorations. "A sweet touch since the whole rescue mission was made possible by bubble gum!"

Cocoa and Melli joined several other Candy Fairies to whip up butterscotch candies.

"I'm so happy this butterscotch didn't go to waste," Cocoa said as she arranged the trays of freshly made candies.

Dash popped a candy into her mouth. "Mmm, you can say that again," she said, licking her lips.

Everyone in Sugar Valley was enjoying the festivities in Caramel Hills. "Nothing like a delicious turn of events," Melli whispered to Raina.

"How sweet it is," she agreed.

A caramella bird landed on Melli's shoulder and nuzzled her neck.

"Hey, little sweets," Melli said, recognizing the yellow bird. "Weren't you covered in butterscotch the last time I saw you?" She rubbed the bird's neck and listened to the soft cooing. "I'm glad you are feeling better," she said. "Now let's try to keep you clean—and safe!"

The bird flew off into Caramel Hills. Melli smiled. She watched her friends enjoying Sun Dip in Caramel Hills. She felt relieved that once again her home was clean.

The quiet and still Butterscotch Volcano stood behind her. She eyed the bubble gum patch on the side. Princess Lolli was right: There was no way to predict another crack or sticky spill. But Melli knew her fairy friends would always be there for her—and the animals. Sure as sugar, Sugar Valley would stick—and work—together.

And that made Melli feel extra-thankful.

"Melli!" Cocoa called. "Everyone is loving our caramel chocolate rolls."

"It feels like ages since we made those," Melli said. "What a long day!"

Cocoa smiled. "Come on, you must try this *butterscotch* hot chocolate. It's double delicious!"

Melli flew over to where her friends and Cara were sitting. She took a cup and Cocoa poured her a serving of the hot, yummy drink. Then Melli raised her cup high in the air. "Here's a toast to bubble gum and to the best team of Candy Fairies!" she said.

The fairies cheered, and everyone enjoyed the sweet drink as the sun settled down behind the Frosted Mountains.

FIND OUT

WHAT HAPPENS IN

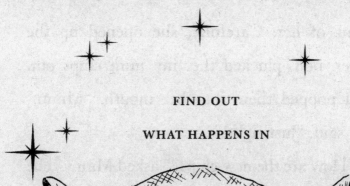

Double Dip

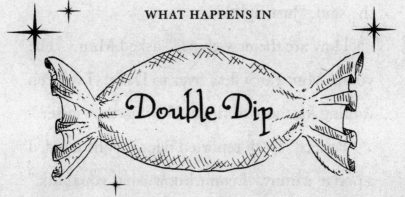

The sweet smell of peppermint made Dash's silver wings flutter. The small Mint Fairy was tending to her candies in Peppermint Grove. The weather was turning a little cooler, and there were many mint candies sprouting on the vines. This was perfect mint-chip weather! Dash picked a tiny mint pod from a stem in front of her. Carefully, she opened up the green pod, plucked the tiny mint chips out, and popped them into her mouth. "Mmm," she said. "Just right!"

"How are the new chips?" asked Minny. The young Mint Fairy flew over to Dash. "I've been waiting for those to ripen. How do they taste?"

"Perfect," Dash reported happily. She handed a pod to Minny. "Let me know what you think."

Minny put a handful of chips in her mouth and quickly agreed. "Yum, these are good," she said. "Dash, you are the master of mint!"

Dash blushed. She was excited about the mini mint chips. She thought they'd be perfect toppings for chocolates or even for ice cream. Just thinking about the yummy treats made her stomach rumble.

"Maybe we should take a break for lunch," Dash suggested. She rubbed her belly. "I'm starving."

Minny laughed. "Dash, you are always hungry!"

Dash couldn't argue. "I might be small, but I do have a huge appetite!" she said, laughing.

There wasn't a candy in Sugar Valley that Dash didn't love . . . although some she liked more than others!

The two Mint Fairies settled down under the shade of a few large peppermint leaves. Dash was thankful for the rest—and the delicious fruit nectar that she had brought for lunch.

"Oh, look, Dash!" Minny exclaimed. "There's a sugar fly note for you." She pointed to the fly circling over Dash's head.

Sugar flies brought messages to fairies throughout Sugar Valley. The flies could spread information—or gossip—to fairies far and wide. Dash quickly opened the note and then flew straight up in the air.

"Holy peppermint!" she cried. She zoomed around and then did a somersault.

"What did that note say?" Minny asked. She leaped up in excitement. "Must be extra-sweet news."

Dash flew back down to the ground. "I just got the best invitation," she told her friend. "You will not believe this. *I* can't believe this!" She shot up in the air again.

"What?" Minny begged. "Come down and tell me!"

"This is *so mint*!" Dash gushed. "Wait till all

my friends hear about this!" She scribbled off a note and handed it back to the sugar fly. "Please take this back to Meringue Island as fast as possible," Dash instructed. "My answer is YES!"

Minny's eyes grew wide. "Meringue Island?" she said. "Why, that's all the way in the Vanilla Sea!"

"Yes," Dash said. "And right near Mount Ice Cream."

Clapping her hands, Minny cheered. "I know—were you invited to race in Double Dip?" she shouted.

"Sure as sugar!" Dash said, flipping in the air again.

"Dash, that is minty cool!" Minny exclaimed. "I've only read about that race. And now you are going to be in it!"

"I can't believe it," Dash repeated, landing back down on the ground.

Minny sighed. "I've never been all the way to Meringue Island," she said wistfully. "I've heard that the Cone Harbor Festival weekend is supersweet. They have all these amazing flavors of ice cream and candy toppings for fairies to taste, and lots of carnival rides and parties." She blushed when Dash raised her eyebrows. "I read all about the festival in the *Daily Scoop*," she confessed.

Dash smiled. "I know. I've read those articles too! The festival seems totally mint," she said. "And I've heard the Double Dip course is one of the most challenging sled races. The race is the last day of the festival."

"Does that mean you'll have to race against

Menta and Peppa?" Minny asked. "They've been the champions for the past two years."

"So you know about those Mint Fairies?" Dash said, raising her eyebrows. "They make mint ice cream and live on Meringue Island. They definitely have an advantage because they've run the course so many times. But this year the race is going to be different."

"Why?" Minny asked, taking a sip of her drink.

"Because this year *I'm* in the race!" Dash boasted proudly. "I've never been to Mount Ice Cream. But now that I've been invited to go, I can't wait! It's not every day that a fairy gets invited to race in Double Dip!" Dash's mind started to flood with ideas. "I can't wait to start working on a new sled. I'll need a double sled for this race," she explained. "And I know just the partner to pick to ride with me."

"Who?" Minny asked. She leaned in closer to Dash.

"The perfect fairy for the job," she said. "She's fearless, and she knows chocolate inside and out."

"Oh, I've read there is that chocolate-coated part of the course," Minny said. She tapped her finger on her head. "I've heard that is the part where lots of fairies fall off their sleds."

"Exactly!" Dash exclaimed. "So with my secret chocolate partner, I'll have the winning edge."

"And a good friend to race with," Minny said, giggling. "I know you are talking about your friend Cocoa. She'll be fantastic."

Taking a bite of a mint, Dash nodded in

agreement. "I hope that she agrees. We'd make a *sugar-tastic* team."

Dash called over another sugar fly. "I wonder if Carobee the dragon would take my friends and me to Meringue Island. The journey would be so sweet on top of a dragon! I hope he will agree to fly us across the Vanilla Sea." She wrote her note and handed it to the sugar fly. "You'll find Carobee in the caves on Meringue Island," Dash told the fly. "Please hurry, and wait for his reply!"

Dash imagined the green-and-purple dragon getting the sugar fly note. She and her friends had met Carobee when they'd been searching for gooey goblins. While they had been looking for the mischievous creatures, they'd found Carobee. The fairies had become fast friends with the dragon after that adventure. Dash hoped that Carobee would be part of this adventure too!

The fly buzzed off toward Meringue Island. Dash leaned back and took a deep, slow breath in and out. "I just know this is going to be my year to win," she said. "To win Double Dip is a huge honor."

"And to beat Menta and Peppa would be a great accomplishment," Minny added.

"Hmm," Dash said, closing her eyes, thinking about the moment of glory. "Can't you see Cocoa and me in the winner's circle?" She sighed. "This is going to be *so mint*!" she exclaimed. "But first I have to ask Cocoa to be my partner!"

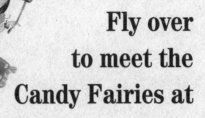

**Fly over
to meet the
Candy Fairies at**

CandyFairies.com

See what the Fairies left behind:

- A sweet eCard to send to your friends
- *Choc-o-rific* activities
- Delicious recipes

**All you need to know about
your favorite characters!**

Mermaid Tales

*Exciting under-the-sea
adventures with Shelly
and her mermaid friends!*

Trouble at Trident Academy

Battle of the Best Friends

A Whale of a Tale

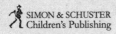

A Valentine's Surprise

Candy Fairies

A Valentine's Surprise

HELEN PERELMAN

ILLUSTRATED BY
ERICA-JANE WATERS

ALADDIN
NEW YORK LONDON TORONTO SYDNEY NEW DELHI

This book is a work of fiction. Any references to historical events, real people, or real locales are used fictitiously. Other names, characters, places, and incidents are the product of the author's imagination, and any resemblance to actual events or locales or persons, living or dead, is entirely coincidental.

ALADDIN

An imprint of Simon & Schuster Children's Publishing Division

1230 Avenue of the Americas, New York, NY 10020

~ First Aladdin paperback edition December 2011

Text copyright © 2011 by Helen Perelman Bernstein

Illustrations copyright © 2011 by Erica-Jane Waters

ALADDIN is a trademark of Simon & Schuster, Inc., and related logo is a registered trademark of Simon & Schuster, Inc.

For information about special discounts for bulk purchases, please contact Simon & Schuster Special Sales at 1-866-506-1949 or business@simonandschuster.com.

The Simon & Schuster Speakers Bureau can bring authors to your live event.

For more information or to book an event contact the Simon & Schuster Speakers Bureau at 1-866-248-3049 or visit our website at www.simonspeakers.com.

Designed by Karina Granda

The text of this book was set in Berthold Baskerville Book.

Manufactured in the United States of America 0113 OFF

4 6 8 10 9 7 5

Library of Congress Control Number 2011920262

ISBN 978-1-4424-2215-5

ISBN 978-1-4424-2216-2 (eBook)

For Sarah Collier, a sweet and true fan

LOLLIPOP LANDING

CANDY CASTLE

FRUIT CHEW MEADOW

RED LICORICE LAKE

PEPPERMINT GROVE

CHOCOLATE

GUMMY FOREST

BLACK LICORICE SWAMP

Contents

1

Supersweet Surprise

Raina the Gummy Fairy sprinkled handfuls of colorful flavor flakes into Gummy Lake. She smiled as the gummy fish swam over and gobbled up the food. Watching the fish eat made Raina's tummy rumble. She had gotten up very early and had been working in Gummy Forest all morning. When she settled on a perch high up on a gummy tree, Raina opened her backpack. All the animals in the forest were fed, and now she could relax and eat her own lunch.

Raina had an important job in Sugar Valley. She took care of the gummy animals that lived in Gummy Forest. There were many types of gummy animals, from friendly bear cubs to playful bunnies. Raina was fair and kind to each of the animals—and they all loved her.

"Hi, Raina!" a voice called out.

Raina looked up to see Dash, a Mint Fairy, flying in circles above her head. The small, sweet fairy glided down to see her.

"I was hoping to find you here," Dash said. "I need your help."

Raina was always willing to help out any

of her friends. She had a heart that was pure sugar. "What's going on?" she asked.

Dash landed on the branch next to Raina. She peered over at the bowl in Raina's hand. Dash was small, but she always had a huge appetite!

"Hmmm, that smells good," she said. "What is that?"

"It's fruit nectar. Berry brought me some yesterday," Raina told her. She watched Dash's eyes grow wider. It wasn't hard to tell that Dash would love a taste. "Do you want to try some?" she asked.

"Thanks," Dash said, licking her lips. "Berry's nectars are always supersweet." Dash leaned over for her taste. Berry the Fruit Fairy had a flair for the fabulous. And she could whip up

4

a spectacular nectar. "Yum," Dash continued. "Berry makes the best fruit nectar soup."

Raina laughed. "I don't think I've ever heard you say that you didn't like something a Candy Fairy made," she told her minty friend.

"Very funny," Dash said, knowing that her friend was speaking the truth.

"Have you come up with any ideas about what to get Berry?" Raina asked.

Dash flapped her wings. "That is why I'm coming to see you," she said. "I was hoping you could give me an idea. I know Berry would love something from Meringue Island, but that is a little too far. She's the only one I haven't gotten a gift for, and Valentine's Day is tomorrow. Since it's also her birthday, I want to make sure the gift is supersweet."

"Sure as sugar, Berry would love anything from Meringue Island," Raina agreed. Meringue Island was in the Vanilla Sea and was *the* place for fashion. Berry loved fashion—especially jewelry and fancy clothes. When Fruli, a Fruit Fairy, had come to Sugar Valley from the island, Berry was very jealous of her. Fruli had beautiful clothes and knew how to put together high-fashion looks.

"The truth is," Raina added, leaning in closer to Dash. "Berry would like anything you gave her."

"But I want to give her something she is really going to love," Dash replied. She swung her legs back and forth. "I want to surprise her with a special gift this year." Her silver wings flapped quickly. "I wish I could think of something with extra sugar!"

"I know how you feel," Raina said. "I've had

the hardest time coming up with an idea." She looked over at Dash. "I'll tell you what I'm going to get her, but please keep it a secret."

"Sure as sugar!" Dash exclaimed. She clapped her hands. "Oh, what are you planning?"

Raina took her last sip of the fruit nectar. "Last night I was reading a story in the Fairy Code Book, and I got a delicious idea."

Dash rolled her eyes. "I should have guessed that this would have something to do with the Fairy Code Book," she said.

Raina read the Fairy Code Book so often that her friends teased her that she knew the whole book by heart.

"Well," Raina continued, "there is a great story in the book about Lyra, the Fruit Chew Meadow unicorn."

"Oh, I love Lyra," Dash sang out. "She grows those gorgeous candy flowers at the edge of the meadow." Just as she said those words, Dash knew why Raina's grin was so wide. "You talked to Lyra, and she is going to give you a special flower for Berry?"

Raina laughed. "Dash!" she said. "You ruined my surprise." She put her empty bowl back inside her bag. "I thought that if I got Berry a flower, I could make a headband for her. You know how she loves to accessorize."

"The more the better, for Berry," Dash added. "And those are the fanciest flowers in the kingdom. *So mint!* Berry is going to love that headband." Dash stopped talking for a moment to take in the whole idea. "Wait, how'd you get

Lyra to do that for you? Unicorns don't like to talk to anyone!"

Raina smiled. "Well, that's not really true," she said.

"Let me guess," Dash said. "Did you read that in a book?"

Raina giggled. "Actually, I didn't," she told her friend. "To be honest, I think Lyra is just shy."

"Really?" Dash asked. "Can I meet her? Maybe she'll have another idea for a gift for Berry. Let's go now." She stood up and leaped off the branch into the air.

"I've been working all morning," Raina said. She reached her arms up into a wide stretch. "Maybe we can go in a little while?"

Dash fluttered back down to the branch. Her

small silver wings flapped quickly. "Come on," she begged. "Let's go now!"

Dash was known for being fast on the slopes of the Frosted Mountains—and for being impatient. She liked to move quickly and make fast decisions.

Leaning back on the gummy tree, Raina closed her eyes. "Please just let me rest a little, and then we can go," she said with a yawn.

"All right," Dash said. "Do you have any more of that nectar?"

Raina gave Dash her bowl and poured out some more of Berry's nectar. Then she shut her eyes. Before Raina drifted off to sleep, she imagined Berry's happy face when she saw her birthday present. Sure as sugar, Valentine's Day was going to be supersweet!

CHAPTER

2

Sweet Lyra

After Raina woke up from her nap, she and Dash flew to Fruit Chew Meadow. The meadow was on the other side of Candy Castle and wasn't that far away from Gummy Forest. Raina knew that with Dash, the trip would go fast. Dash was a champion at sledding and loved to fly down the slopes of the Frosted Mountains and

Marshmallow Marsh on her sled. Raina usually preferred to take her time. She liked to see the colorful sights Sugar Valley and enjoy all the delicious scents blowing in the breeze. Today, however, she was ready to race Dash to Fruit Chew Meadow.

"I can't believe I'm keeping up with you," Raina called over to Dash.

Dash smiled. "I'm glad you *are* going fast. I can't wait to talk to Lyra!"

Laughing, Raina shook her head. Her minty friend always wanted a speedy answer. Raina flapped her wings. She was excited to see the flower that Lyra had for her.

"I thought unicorns were a little sticky when it came to being around fairies," Dash said.

"Not Lyra," Raina said. "She's not like that

at all. Besides, Lyra likes Berry very much. She wants to help make her birthday special."

"Berry is going to be so happy!" Dash said, smiling.

Now that Candy Castle was behind them, Fruit Chew Meadow was just ahead. The fairies flapped their wings faster and giggled as they headed toward the ground. As they drew closer, Raina stopped laughing and squinted her eyes. Normally, the far end of Fruit Chew Meadow was full of flowers. The bright rainbow of colorful flowers was always such a breathtaking sight. But today the field looked different.

"Oh no!" Raina gasped. Her wings slowed as she glided above the meadow. Usually, the tall candy flowers were reaching up to the sky, but now they were dragging on the ground.

"Holy peppermint," Dash mumbled as she flew closer to the field. "These flowers look awful."

"What happened?" Raina said. She hovered above the ground, staring at the sad-looking flowers. "This must have just happened. We would have heard of this for sure."

"Sour news travels fast," Dash agreed. "I'm sure Princess Lolli doesn't even know about this, otherwise she would be here now."

Princess Lolli was the fairy princess who ruled over Sugar Valley. She was fair and true and always helped out the fairies when there was trouble.

"I wonder if anyone else knows about this," Dash said. She spun around. "Do you see Lyra anywhere?"

Raina held her hand over her eyes to shield the sun. She scanned the meadow. "I don't see her. We have to find her." She flapped her wings and flew up to see better. "Lyra's usually right here near the berry cherry tree," she said. "I wonder where she could be." She looked over at Dash.

"I don't have a good feeling about this," Dash said. She wrinkled her nose. "Something smells sour here."

"Well," Raina said, trying to stay calm. "Let's look for clues. That's always the best way to solve a mystery."

The two fairies hovered above the meadow and searched.

"Poor Lyra," Dash said. "This must have happened after all the Fruit Fairies left this morning."

Raina nodded. "You must be right," she said. "The Fruit Fairies would have helped. Keep looking!"

As Raina flew over the meadow she wasn't sure what she was looking for. Lyra was a large white unicorn with a rainbow horn that glowed. There weren't many places for an animal that size to hide in the meadow.

"Wait!" Raina said. She flew down to the ground and squatted low on the grass. Dash followed close behind her.

"Lyra's hoofprints!" Raina exclaimed. She pointed to a dirt path and a small hoofprint. "If we follow these, maybe we can find her."

The two fairies followed the hoofprint clues. Near the edge of the meadow they found the unicorn.

"Oh, Lyra!" Raina cried out. She saw the beautiful white unicorn lying down behind a berry thistle and rushed toward her.

Lyra was lying on her side. Her normally bright rainbow horn was dull and nearly wiped of color.

Raina sat by Lyra's head and stroked her nose. "Lyra, are you okay?" she whispered softly in her ear.

There was no answer.

"Lyra," Raina begged. "Please answer me. What happened?"

Dash sat down on the other side of Lyra's head. She rubbed her silky white neck. "Lyra, can you hear us?" she asked.

Lyra's eyes fluttered slightly.

"She looks very weak," Dash added. "Poor

Lyra!" She bent down to get a closer look at the unicorn. "She's really sick."

Raina knew they had to do something—and fast. It was hard to tell just how long Lyra had been lying there. And her dull horn was very upsetting. "We need all of us together to solve this problem," she said.

Lyra's eyes fluttered again. The unicorn's long lashes seemed too heavy to let her keep her eyes open.

"It's all right," Raina told her. She patted Lyra gently. "We're going to get you some help," she whispered in her ear.

"And try to figure out what went on here," Dash added.

Raina stood up and looked around. The field seemed so strange without the tall stalks of colorful flowers. "Maybe she hurt herself," she said softly. She looked over Lyra's white body, but the unicorn appeared unharmed.

"We can't move her by ourselves," Dash said. Lyra was a full-sized unicorn and much too large for just two Candy Fairies to pick up.

Raina knew Dash was right. "Let's send sugar flies to our friends. If we're all together, we can come up with a plan."

The fastest way to get information around Sugar Valley was to send a sugar fly note. Those little flies could spread news faster than anyone.

Poor, sweet Lyra, Raina thought. *How did this happen to you?*

Raina touched the unicorn's horn and closed her eyes. She wished she could help the gentle creature and find out what had made her so sick.

CHAPTER
3

A Sour Mystery

Raina and Dash sat by Lyra's side. The unicorn seemed to be resting, but she was weak and her horn was still dull. Raina didn't like seeing the unicorn so sick.

"Let's try to make Lyra more comfortable," Raina said. She gathered some soft fruit chews and put them under Lyra's head. "Oh, I hope the others get here soon!" she said, looking up at the sky.

"Let's tell everyone that we were working on a special candy for Princess Lolli," Dash said. "I don't want to give away Berry's surprise gift. She'll figure out that we were up to something."

"Maybe," Raina said. "But then there will be questions about the special candy." She reached over and pet Lyra. She felt very warm. "Telling one little lie doesn't seem bad, but one lie always leads to many, many more."

Dash agreed. "You're right. We'll just say that we came to see Lyra. Everyone will be thinking about how to help her."

Putting her head close to Lyra's nose, Raina listened carefully. "She's barely breathing," she told Dash.

"Look!" Dash cried. "I see Melli and Cocoa!"

Up in the sky the Caramel Fairy and Chocolate Fairy were headed toward them. Raina waved. Just as they landed Berry flew in beside them.

"Sour strawberries!" Berry exclaimed. "What happened here?" She bent down to Lyra. "I was just here this morning and Lyra was fine. Oh, the poor thing." Gently she stroked the sleeping unicorn's neck.

"Sweet Lyra," Melli sighed.

"She doesn't look well," Cocoa added. She glanced around at all the wilted flowers in the meadow. "Melli and I were nearby around lunchtime, and the flowers were standing tall. So Lyra couldn't have been lying here for long."

"Oh, Lyra," Berry cooed. She sat down close

to her. "Sour sugars! Look at her horn!" Berry looked at Raina. "Her magic!"

"We have to get her some help," Raina said. She was trying very hard to remain calm.

"Unicorns hold all their magic in their horn," Berry blurted out. "Lyra must be very sick if her horn is so dull."

Raina lowered her eyes. She was aware of that fact, but she had been too worried to say those words out loud.

Melli paced around Lyra. "Oh, this is awful. And a mystery."

"A sour mystery," Dash mumbled.

Cocoa flew up in the air and scanned the meadow. "All of Lyra's flowers are drooping. Whatever is affecting her is affecting the whole meadow."

"The flowers respond to Lyra," Berry said. "If she doesn't have her magic and she can't sing, the flowers will die." Berry's wings began to move. "We have to do something fast."

Raina put her hand on Berry's shoulder. "That is why we called you all here."

"Let me stay with Lyra," Berry said. She reached in her bag for some fruit nectar. "Maybe she'll have some." She held the food out to the unicorn, but there was no movement.

"She's so weak," Melli said sadly.

Raina's eyes were brimming with tears. She knew that she had to be strong. "Berry, you stay with Lyra and keep her calm. The rest of us will search the meadow. We'll look for clues."

The fairies all agreed. Berry stayed with Lyra as Raina, Dash, Melli, and Cocoa flew back and forth over the meadow. Overall, the meadow didn't look disturbed . . . except for the wilted flowers.

"Holy peppermint!" Dash cried out. She waved her friends over to the edge of the meadow. She zoomed down to the ground and then signaled her friends to follow.

"A broken fence!" Raina exclaimed. She landed beside Dash, the others right behind her.

The thick caramel fence surrounding one of the flower beds was broken.

"Those fences are incredibly strong," Melli said. She bent down to examine the break. "That caramel is hard to crack."

Cocoa ducked down low to get a better view. "Well, something—or someone—broke the fence."

Dash sat down on the ground and put her head in her hands. As she stared at the broken fence her nose began to twitch. She put her hand on the ground and then up to her mouth. "Holy peppermint!" she said softly. "There's salt all over the ground here." She stood up and began to follow the path while the others watched her with puzzled expressions. Suddenly Dash bent down, scooped something up in her hand, and then she showed it to her friends.

"Salt?" Melli asked. "How could there be salt here? Everyone knows . . ."

Before she could finish her sentence, her friends were around her. Melli had her hand in front of her mouth. She couldn't bear to say the words.

"Salt is poisonous for unicorns!" Raina blurted out.

"Mogu! That salty old troll," Cocoa hissed.

"No wonder Lyra is weak and sick," Melli said softly.

Dash was so angry her wings flapped and took her up off the ground. "Mogu has been coming to the meadow to steal candy! And his salty tracks have harmed Lyra. This is so sour—even for Mogu."

"You really think Mogu would hurt Lyra?" Raina asked. "Even for a troll that would be superbitter."

"Maybe he didn't realize the salt was harmful to Lyra," Melli offered.

"Not likely," Cocoa muttered. "He saw a broken fence as an invitation."

"Sweet sugar," Raina gasped. "We need to get Lyra stronger so that she can sing and get back to guarding the meadow." She looked at her friends. "And we need to tell Berry. She's not going to handle this well."

"And Berry's birthday is tomorrow," Melli added sadly. "This doesn't seem like a time for celebrating at all."

Raina took a deep breath. "Dash and I came here to get one of Lyra's flowers so we could make Berry's birthday gift extra-sweet." Raina looked over at Fruit Chew Meadow and sighed. "We still have time to solve this mystery and to make Berry's birthday *and* Valentine's Day special." She looked at the worried expressions on her friends' faces. "We have to at least try."

4

A Salty Problem

When the four friends returned to the far end of Fruit Chew Meadow, Berry was still sitting next to Lyra. The unicorn had not moved since they had left. Berry was stroking Lyra's neck and singing softly.

"Gentle breeze and sweet light," Berry sang out,

"How is Lyra?" Raina asked, kneeling beside her friend. The white unicorn was still asleep and her horn was still dull. Not a trace was visible of the colors that normally glowed from her horn. "Did she wake up?"

"Yes, she took a few sips of the nectar but then dozed off again," Berry said. "Did you find any clues?"

Raina decided not to sugarcoat the truth. "We found a broken fence and a trail of salt," she told her.

"Salt?!" Berry exclaimed. Her eyes were wide and full of concern.

Raina knew that Berry was aware of the dangers of salt in the meadow.

"Oh, this is worse than we thought," Berry said softly. She looked into Raina's eyes. "It's Mogu, isn't it?"

"We're not sure," Raina told Berry. "But the first thing we need to do is get rid of the salt. If we can clear the area, maybe Lyra will be able to speak to us and tell us what happened."

"Let's try to wash all the flowers off," Berry said.

Raina smiled at her Fruit Fairy friend. "That's what I thought too. We'll make a spring rain to take the salt away. We can go to Red Licorice Lake for the water."

"I'll stay with Lyra," Berry offered. She looked down at the gentle unicorn. "She seems to do better when I sing to her."

Raina gave her friend a quick hug. "That is a great idea," she said. "You stay here."

The four fairies flew down to the shores of Red Licorice Lake. They each grabbed a bucket from a nearby shed. Buckets were kept there in case of droughts or other emergencies.

This is definitely an emergency, thought Raina.

"Once the salt is gone, Lyra will feel better, right?" Dash asked Raina as she filled up her bucket.

"I hope so," Raina replied. She didn't know for sure, but she knew that the salt was causing Lyra to grow weak and sick. "Come, let's hurry," she urged her friends.

Together, the fairies flew up and down the meadow. They poured the water over the wilted

flowers and washed the white salt away. With each trip to the lake, the salt was slowly disappearing. It took many trips and bucketfuls of water, but soon the wet meadow didn't have a trace of salt.

Then the fairies gathered back around Lyra and Berry.

"How is Lyra?" Raina asked as they flew up.

"She's a little better," Berry told her. "Getting rid of the salt has helped. I can see she's a little stronger."

"This still doesn't make sense to me," Raina said. She sat down next to Berry, tapping her finger to her head. "Mogu is afraid of Lyra. Why would he even come here?"

"Who would be afraid of a sweet unicorn?" Dash asked.

"When it comes to Mogu, there isn't always a solid reason," Berry told her.

"I remember those tall stalks of salty pretzels in Black Licorice Swamp," Cocoa told her friends. "If there is salt here, I'm sure it's because of Mogu and the Chuchies."

Raina knew that Cocoa was remembering the time when she flew to Black Licorice Swamp. Mogu and his mischievous companions, the Chuchies, had stolen her chocolate eggs. Cocoa had tricked Mogu into giving them back. The Chocolate Fairy knew all about the troll's salty ways.

"If there is salt here, Mogu is probably to blame," Cocoa said again. "His greed will drive him to do anything." Thinking of her chocolate eggs made Cocoa stamp her foot. "We have to trick Mogu again," she said. "Cleaning up the meadow may solve the problem for now, but that troll will be back."

"Especially if Lyra isn't guarding the flowers," Melli added. "There's nothing here to stop him."

"We're here now," Raina said bravely. "It's sticky business to trick a troll," she reminded her friends. She reached into her bag. "I know I've heard a story about Mogu and Lyra. Maybe there's a clue in a story that can help us."

Raina took out her Fairy Code Book and thumbed through the pages.

Dash sat down next to her. "I can't imagine Mogu being afraid of anything."

Flipping through the book, Raina agreed. "Yes, yes, I'm sure I've read a story in here about Mogu and Lyra. I think it was about Lyra's pointy horn."

Laughing, Berry slapped her hand to her knee. "I bet that horn can come in handy when dealing with Mogu," she said, giggling.

"What is the story?" Dash asked. She was growing impatient.

"Mogu was once pricked by Lyra's horn when he tried to steal her fruit-chew flowers," Raina read from the thick book. She turned the book around to show her friends the picture. "I knew there was a story!"

"Ha!" Dash burst out. "Look at that!" She pointed to a picture of Mogu with a tear in his pants. Sticking out of the hole was Mogu's polka-dotted underwear. "No wonder Mogu is afraid of Lyra. She totally embarrassed him!"

"You should really read the Fairy Code Book more often," Raina scolded her friends.

"We don't have to," Berry said, smiling. "We have you! You remember every story."

Melli put her arm around Raina. "And it's a good thing, too," she said. "Raina, what would we do without you?"

Blushing, Raina turned the page. "This was many years ago, and Mogu has not been back here since. I wonder what made him come back now."

"Maybe he just wanted to have a fruit-chew flower," Berry offered. "They are the sweetest in Sugar Valley."

Raina looked over at Dash. She didn't want her to say anything about the gift for Berry. She caught Dash's eye. Dash immediately understood and bit her lip. It was hard for Dash not to speak her mind!

"Or maybe he heard about the broken fence

and thought he could slip in unnoticed," Dash said.

"Who knows why a salty old troll does anything," Melli said. She got up and paced around in a circle.

Berry rubbed Lyra's dull horn. "Lyra needs help," she said. "Cleaning the meadow is not going to wash this problem away."

Raina hugged the Fairy Code Book close to her chest. Normally, reading a story helped her decide the right thing to do. But this tale offered little advice. All she knew for sure was that Lyra was not better. Berry was right, just washing the meadow wasn't going to solve the problem. If they were going to help Lyra, they had to come up with a plan to stop Mogu. And to get Lyra well again.

And that was a salty problem she had no idea how to solve.

5

Burst of Hope

Raina and Berry huddled together on a blanket in Fruit Chew Meadow. Normally, Raina would have loved to spend time hanging out with Berry. Only now they were both worried about Lyra. Lyra had been resting under Berry's pink cotton-candy shawl, but she still looked very weak. The others had flown off to get some food for dinner. Raina was having a hard time keeping still. Her wings were fluttering and she was twisting her long hair around her finger.

"You're worried about Lyra, aren't you?" Berry asked.

"Yes," Raina said. But she couldn't tell Berry that Lyra was not all she was concerned about. She also didn't want to ruin Berry's birthday with this sour event. With the look of things now, it didn't seem that Lyra would be getting better by Sun Dip. Normally, Sun Dip was a festive time of day when fairies would gather. The sun would slide behind the Frosted Mountains and the sky would turn deep pinks and purples. Fairies would share sweet treats and talk with friends. But today when the sun went down, there'd be little Raina and her friends would want to celebrate.

Raina touched the Fairy Code Book in her bag. She wished the story about Mogu and Lyra had helped her come up with a plan. She sighed.

"Mogu has a way of ruining sweet times in Sugar Valley," Berry said softly. She leaned forward to pet Lyra. "Please, Lyra, take some nectar. It will make your throat feel better. We all need you to sing."

Raina blew her bangs off her forehead. Lyra was not getting stronger, even though all the salt had been washed away. They were going to have to move her. "How are we going to move a unicorn?" Raina asked.

"We've brought food," Cocoa called from above.

"I'm not really hungry," Raina replied.

"Me neither," Berry told Cocoa.

Cocoa, Melli, and Dash came to sit on the blanket. They spread out the food for their friends.

"We should eat," Melli said. "Then we can think of a solid plan."

Dash looked around at the pale, wilted flowers. "What do you think will happen to the flowers if Lyra's voice doesn't come back?" she asked.

Raina lowered her head. "I'm not sure," she said. "I don't think the flowers will survive. Already they look even less colorful, and it's only been a few hours."

"The greatest present for my birthday would be if Lyra would get better," Berry mumbled.

Hoping that she could make her friend's wish come true, Raina gave Berry a tight squeeze.

"We still have time," she said, trying to believe her words would come true.

A gentle breeze ruffled the grass. Above them Raina spotted a sweet sight. "Oh, Berry!" she cried out. "It's Princess Lolli!"

In a flash, Princess Lolli was standing before them. Her long strawberry-blond hair hung down at her shoulders, and a small candy-jeweled tiara sat on top of her head. She smoothed her bright pink dress with her hands and smiled at the young fairies. "Hello, fairies," she said. "I heard that Lyra is not well. I am so glad you are here with her."

"I don't think we've helped her much," Berry said sadly. "She is still very weak."

"Lyra can't sing," Raina said, stepping forward. "We found a broken fence and salt. We washed

the flowers and tried to get Lyra to drink some nectar. Nothing seems to be working."

"Salt?" Princess Lolli said. Her smile melted into a frown. "I was afraid that was the case."

"Do you think Mogu was here?" Cocoa asked.

"I'm not sure," the princess said. "I do know that Lyra needs some help. Let's get her to Candy Castle."

Raina bent down low to Lyra. "She can't even open her eyes. She's so weak," she said. "Lyra can't fly. How can we get her to Candy Castle?"

Everyone looked at one another.

"Bitter mint," Dash mumbled. "This is a super minty problem. Without Lyra's glowing horn, she can't fly. She's out of the race."

"That's it!" Raina shouted. Her wings flapped happily, and she rushed over to give Dash a hug.

"What?" Dash gasped.

Raina grinned at her friend. "I know exactly what we need to do," she told her friends. "I'm sure this will work!"

For the first time since they had arrived at Fruit Chew Meadow, Raina suddenly had a burst of hope.

6

Sweet and Strong

Raina was grinning while her friends gazed at her. Their mouths were open and their eyes wide.

"You really think that will work?" Cocoa asked.

Melli bit her lower lip. "Sweet caramel, Raina," she muttered. "I'm not sure we could pull that off."

"Sure as sugar, we can!" Raina exclaimed. She stood up straight, with her hands on her hips. "We have Dash, the best sled racer in Sugar Valley. We'll make a sled mint enough for a sweet unicorn. If Lyra can't fly, we'll have to pull her to Candy Castle."

Princess Lolli smiled. "Raina, that is an excellent idea," she said. "If there are any fairies who can make this happen, I believe those fairies are right here in front of me now."

"What about Mogu?" Dash asked. "What if he comes back?"

"We'll have to wait to deal with Mogu," Princess Lolli told the fairies. "First we must help Lyra." She bent down to the unicorn and whispered in her ear. Lyra slowly opened her eyes. Princess Lolli took a pink sugar cube from her

pocket and held it out to Lyra. The unicorn took the sweet treat and then closed her eyes again. Standing up, Princess Lolli faced the fairies. "I will head back to the castle to make arrangements for Lyra. I will see you all shortly."

The fairies waved good-bye to Princess Lolli. They were so thankful that she had come, but now they had work to do! If they were going to build a sled big enough for a unicorn, they had to work quickly.

Raina opened the Fairy Code Book. She put the book down on the ground for everyone to see. "Look, there's a picture of a large sled," she said. "This sled was for Mooco the chocolate cow, when she was stuck in the terrible winter storm last year in Chocolate Woods." She held up the book to show her friends the illustration.

"Hot chocolate!" Cocoa shouted. "I remember that storm. That poor cow was stuck in the thick frozen chocolate. It took every Chocolate Fairy's help to get her out."

"I think we can use this picture of a large sled to help us," Raina said. "If the Chocolate Fairies could move Mooco, we can move Lyra." She turned to Dash. "What do you think? Can we make a sled big enough for Lyra?"

Dash leaned over to see the picture. "Sure as sugar," she replied. She smiled at Raina. "Just as Princess Lolli said, we are the fairies for the job!"

Raina was thankful for the Mint Fairy's enthusiasm. She knew she could always count on Dash.

"We'll need a few supplies," Dash said. She started to pace back and forth as she thought out loud. "We'll need some fruit leather, red licorice, and something to hold the sled together."

"What about hot caramel?" Melli asked. "When the sticky syrup dries, it should hold the sled together."

"Thanks, Melli. I think you're right," Dash said. "The hot caramel is a smart choice."

Berry leaped up. "I can get the fruit leather," she said. "We'll need wide strips, and I know where to get good, strong pieces."

"I can get the licorice," Cocoa offered.

"I'll head to the Frosted Mountains to get the frosting for the tips of the sled," Dash told her friends. "If we are going to pull the sled, we'll need to make sure the blades are smooth enough to glide over the ground." Her wings fluttered and she shot up in the air. "This sled is going to be *so mint*!"

Raina knew her friends would come together to make this happen. "I'll stay here and keep Lyra comfortable," she said. "Dash, do you think we'll be able to get Lyra to the castle before Sun Dip?"

"Yes," she said, "I do." Then she smiled. "I'm not sure we'll win any races, but we can get Lyra there before dark."

The fairies all flew off to get their supplies. Before the sun reached the very top of the mountains, the fairies were back at Fruit Chew Meadow.

True to Dash's promise, she built a sled with all the materials her friends had gathered. Soon they had a sled large enough for a unicorn in the meadow.

Melli and Berry held up the licorice ropes.

"We braided them to make them stronger," Melli said.

"Sweet and strong," Dash said. "I should get you all to work on my next sled with me." She attached the frosted licorice blades to the sled and then stood back to admire the finished product. "Not bad," she said, checking over the sled. "I think we're about done."

Raina was feeding Lyra tiny bits of rainbow gummy chews when she heard Dash's news. Lyra's horn was still dull and the unicorn had not spoken or sung a word. Raina tried not to show her concern, but she was very worried.

"The sled is finished," Dash said.

The five fairies surrounded Lyra. They each took a piece of the blanket she was lying on and gently lifted the unicorn to the sled. Dash had done a great job of measuring the seat. The sled was perfect for Lyra.

"Sour sugars," Raina gasped. She pointed to Lyra's horn. Instead of being dull, the horn was now black. "We have to get her to Candy Castle right away!"

A Sweet Ride

"Grab hold!" Raina instructed as she tossed the licorice ropes out to her friends.

The fairies worked together to pull the large sled through Fruit Chew Meadow. Each of them held on tight to the braided red licorice ropes and pulled with all her might. As they passed Red Licorice Lake, no one spoke a word. Each fairy was concentrating on pulling the sled—and getting the sick unicorn to the castle.

"Not much farther," Raina called over her shoulder. Glancing back at Lyra, she saw that the unicorn was resting comfortably on the sled. Only her horn made her seem different. Raina didn't have to look *that* fact up in the Fairy Code Book. A dull black horn was not a sign of a healthy unicorn.

"Dash, this sled is smooth as caramel," Melli said. "I can't believe we are pulling Lyra all the way to the castle."

"This is one smooth, sweet ride," Berry added.

Up ahead Raina saw the tall sugar cube walls of Candy Castle come into view. Never had Raina been so happy to see the pink-and-white sugarcoated castle! If anyone could save the unicorn, it was Princess Lolli.

As the fairies neared the front gate the castle guards came out to greet them. Quickly the guards took over and pulled Lyra through the gates into the Royal Gardens. They had been expecting the sick unicorn, and they were ready for her.

Princess Lolli came out to the garden. "I knew you would get Lyra here," she said to the fairies. She took a step back to admire the sled they had built. "This is extraordinary!"

"We all worked together," Raina spoke up. She turned to smile at Dash. "But this was Dash's design."

Dash blushed. "Sure as sugar, it helped to

have a Caramel, Gummy, Fruit, and Chocolate Fairy around," she said.

The fairy princess laughed. "Well done," she said. "And we are all so grateful." She waved her hand toward the large front door. "Come, let's get Lyra inside. We have a special vanilla bath waiting for her."

"Will she be all right?" Raina asked. She watched as the sled was pulled inside the castle. "Her horn has turned black," she said in a hushed voice.

Princess Lolli put her arm around Raina. "Yes, I saw that," she said gently. "I was worried that might happen. But now that Lyra is here, we'll be able to help her. The vanilla bath will get rid of any trace of salt." She smiled at Raina. "Lyra is going to be fine. Your getting her here quickly saved her."

Raina lowered her head. If only she had gotten to Fruit Chew Meadow earlier! She should have listened to Dash. If she had, they would have found Lyra sooner. And maybe the unicorn would not be this ill.

"Raina, this isn't your fault," Berry whispered in her ear. She came up beside her friend when she saw the worried look on Raina's face. "The important thing is that we got Lyra here to the castle. Now she can get help."

Hearing Berry say this to her made Raina feel worse. She should not have taken that nap after lunch. She and Dash could have been in the meadow to stop Mogu.

Dash flew over to Raina and gently pulled her away from the others. "Mogu stirred up trouble long before we got to Fruit Chew Meadow," she told her. "Berry is right. At least now Lyra is safe here at the castle."

"But I . . . ," Raina started to say. Tears gathered in her eyes.

Holding up her hand, Dash cut Raina off. "No one is more considerate of the animals in Sugar Valley than you," she said firmly. "Please don't be upset. If we're going to get Fruit Chew Meadow back to normal, we have to get Mogu out of there tonight. We can do it."

"Thank you, Dash," Raina said. She wiped away her tears and took a deep breath. "I guess

the important thing now is to find a way to keep that salty troll out of the meadow."

"And those Chuchies," Dash grumbled.

"How about we fix the fence first?" Melli called over to her friends. "We have leftover caramel from the sled already at the meadow. We can use that to patch up the hole."

"If this is Mogu's work," Raina said, "a fence won't keep him out. Fences don't keep trolls out." She sat down under a gummy tree in the Royal Gardens. "We need to find a way to trick Mogu—or at least teach him a lesson."

"I had a feeling she was going to say that," Dash said, smiling. She sat down next to Raina.

"He can't keep bringing salt into the meadow," Melli said. "You'd think that he'd notice the damage he's done to the flowers and Lyra."

"Mogu only cares about himself," Cocoa told her friends.

"Too bad we don't know another unicorn with a rainbow horn," joked Berry. "That would make Mogu jump."

Raina flew straight up in the air. Her wings were moving as fast as the thoughts in her head. "I know how we can trick that salty troll!" Raina shouted. "First I need to get something from Gummy Forest. I'll meet you all back at Fruit Chew Meadow at the end of Sun Dip."

Before her friends could ask any questions, Raina raced off to Gummy Forest. She hoped with all her heart that her plan to trick Mogu would work. She never wanted to see Lyra looking so sick again. And she had a few hours left to save Berry's birthday—and Valentine's Day!

8

A Gummy Good Idea

Raina sped through Gummy Forest. The sun was heading quickly toward the top of the Frosted Mountains. She didn't have much time! Raina worked quickly and gathered all she needed for her plan. She had to get back to Fruit Chew Meadow before dark.

This has to trick Mogu, she thought. If she could

get Mogu and the Chuchies out of the meadow, the flowers would bounce back by morning and the meadow would be safe for Lyra. The fairies could celebrate Lyra's return—and Berry's birthday. This was a delicious plan!

The gummy cubs and bunnies watched Raina work. They were curious about what the Gummy Fairy was doing and crowded around her.

"Sweet sugar cubes!" Raina exclaimed. She looked over at the group of gummy animals. "What do you think?" A smile spread across her face as she held up her work.

The animals were not sure what Raina was creating, but they sensed it was exactly what she had set out to make.

"Oh, I hope this works," Raina said to the animals. She reached over to pet a blue gummy

bear on the head. "Be good, Blue Belle," she said. "Look after the others for me. I will be back soon."

When Raina arrived at Fruit Chew Meadow, the sky was a deep lavender with spots of pink swirls. Normally, Raina loved Sun Dip. She enjoyed talking to her friends, telling stories, and sampling the candy crops of the day. Only today Sun Dip was not about having fun. Today Sun Dip was about tricking a troll!

"Are you ready to teach Mogu a lesson?" Raina asked as she touched down next to her friends. They were all waiting near the berry cherry tree.

"Sure as sugar!" Berry replied.

"We mended the fence with hot caramel," Melli said. "Mogu will have a harder time getting into the meadow now."

Raina took her gummy creation out of her

bag. She held up the rainbow gummy unicorn horn proudly. "This should keep Mogu and the Chuchies out for a long, long time," she said.

Melli gasped. "Where'd you get that?"

"Is . . . is . . . is that Lyra's horn?" Dash asked. Her mouth hung open and her eyes were wide with disbelief.

"No, silly," Raina said. "It's a gummy cone from a pine gummy tree," she told her friends. She smiled slyly. "And then I added a little more gummy candy."

"Lickin' lollipops, Raina!" Berry exclaimed. "That looks just like Lyra's horn!"

Raina's wings fluttered. She blushed a little too. "I was hoping you'd say that," she admitted. "The real test is if Mogu and the Chuchies think this is really Lyra's horn."

"What are you planning?" Cocoa asked.

Leaning in toward her friends, Raina spoke softly. "I was thinking if we hid in the bushes and poked this horn out, Mogu would get spooked that Lyra is back." She raised her eyebrows. "What do you think?"

"Holy peppermint!" Dash burst out. "You are *so mint*, Raina."

Her friends all nodded in agreement.

"It's a gummy good idea!" Cocoa blurted out.

Raina was glad her friends thought her idea would work. She hoped the horn would fool Mogu and the Chuchies.

The five fairies crept along the hedges lining the edge of the meadow. They didn't have to wait long. Soon they saw Mogu and the Chuchies approaching the gate. As they got closer Raina felt her stomach flip-flop. Seeing Mogu in his clunky boots caked with salt made her so mad.

"Just look at him," Berry snarled. "He doesn't even care that the salt on his boots made Lyra sick."

Dash popped up in between Raina and Berry. "Maybe he didn't know?" she asked.

Raina watched the grumpy, greedy troll. His big belly hung over his pants, and his white hair stuck up in a ring around his huge head. "He doesn't seem very concerned about anyone but himself—and his tummy."

"Well, look at this!" Mogu grumbled. He stopped in front of the mended fence. "Seems someone fixed the fence." He stuck his chocolate-stained fingers into the caramel patch, which had not dried yet.

"Yummmm," he said, licking his finger. "Fresh caramel is *sooooooo* good."

Melli's face turned a bright cherry red. She bit her lip so she would keep quiet.

Raina hunched down low and rustled the leaves in the bushes. Now was the time to get this show started! She slipped the gummy horn onto a stick.

"Meeeeeeeeeeee, meeeeee!" the Chuchies shouted, jumping up and down on their short, skinny legs. Their furry, round yellow bodies shook as they jumped.

"Shhhh," snapped Mogu. He held his hand up to quiet the Chuchies. Looking around, he narrowed his eyes. "What was that?" he asked.

"Meeeeeeeee, meeeeee?" the Chuchies asked.

Raina rustled the bush branches again.

"Couldn't be," Mogu muttered. He pushed down on the caramel fence where the caramel was still soft, and he broke through.

Holding tight, Raina swayed the rainbow gummy pinecone around. Then she stuck the horn through the bush.

"Salty sticks!" Mogu exclaimed. "How can that be?" He rubbed his eyes. The light was fading fast. "She's back?"

Raina looked over at Berry. Now was her time to sing! Berry nodded and smiled at Raina.

"Gentle breeze and sweet light, flavors of the rainbow grow bright . . . ," Berry sang out.

Raina was impressed by how similar Berry sounded to Lyra. As she sang Raina moved the horn just as if Lyra was there. When Berry finished the song, Dash popped her head up over the bush.

"They're leaving!" Dash cried.

All the fairies peered over the bush. Raina couldn't believe her eyes. Mogu and the Chuchies were running away!

9

Three Delicious Reasons

Are they really gone?" Raina asked. She squinted her eyes to see in the early evening dim light.

"Yes!" Dash cheered. "The gummy pinecone trick worked!"

"Raina, that was *choc-o-rific!*" Cocoa blurted out. "You fooled Mogu."

Melli fluttered her wings and lifted off the ground. "And I don't think he'll be coming back anytime soon," she added. "I didn't think that Mogu could move that fast."

"Oh, we have to let Lyra know," Berry said. "I can't wait to see the look on her face." She turned to Raina. "Thank you. On behalf of all the Fruit Fairies—and all Candy Fairies—thank you!"

"Do you want us to go with you?" Melli asked.

Berry shook her head. "No, I'll go," she told her friends. "I feel bad that I wasn't here earlier to help Lyra. I was at Lollipop Landing this morning, and I wish I had been here." She lowered her head and fingered her fruit-chew bracelet. "If I'd been here, I would have been able to stop Mogu, and Lyra wouldn't be so sick."

At that moment Raina realized that she wasn't the only one feeling responsible for Lyra's misfortune. When something so sour happened, everyone felt bad.

"You know," Raina said to her friend, "we all feel responsible. I was thinking that if I had come earlier to the meadow, I could have stopped Mogu too."

Berry looked up at Raina.

"Me too," Dash said.

"We were thinking the same thing," Melli said, pointing at herself and Cocoa.

"I guess the important thing is that we did get here," Raina told them. "Lyra is getting help and Mogu is gone."

A smile appeared on Berry's face. "You're right," she said. "Thank you." She sniffed a little.

"I'll see you tomorrow. Red Licorice Lake for Sun Dip?"

"It's a plan," Raina said, giving her friend a hug.

As Berry headed off to Candy Castle, Raina looked around at Dash, Cocoa, and Melli.

"I think Berry forgot that tomorrow is her birthday!" she said. "What do you think of having a surprise party in Fruit Chew Meadow?" Raina saw her friends grinning. "It will be a triply sweet celebration—a homecoming for Lyra, a birthday party for Berry, and a Valentine's Day surprise for all Candy Fairies."

"Berry will love the idea," Cocoa said.

"She deserves a supersweet surprise for her birthday," Melli added.

A sugar fly landed on Raina's shoulder. The envelope was from Princess Lolli.

Princess Lolli
Candy Castle
Sugar Valley
Candy Kingdom

Lyra is doing well.
She enjoyed her
vanilla bath, and her
horn is back to normal.
She is going to be fine.
Many thanks to you and
your friends,
Princess Lolli.

"This must be news about Lyra," Raina said, opening up the note. "Dash, could you hold up a mint stick so I can read this? I hope this is good news."

Dash held up a bright mint stick as the fairies huddled around Raina. They were anxious to hear the royal news.

"Lyra is doing well," Raina read. "She enjoyed

her vanilla bath, and her horn is back to normal. She is going to be fine. Many thanks to you and your friends, Princess Lolli."

"So mint!" Dash exclaimed. "Now we definitely need to plan a celebration."

Raina took out a notebook from her bag. "We don't have much time to pull this party together. So we'll have to be fast." She started making a list. "First we need to try to keep this a secret. Part of the fun will be surprising Berry."

"And Lyra," Cocoa added.

Tapping her pen on her notebook, Raina tried to think of all the ingredients for a good party. "First, we need to send out invites with the sugar flies. We'll have to make sure to write Top Secret so no one tells Berry about the party."

Melli peered over Raina's shoulder to look at her list. "How are we ever going to pull this party together by Sun Dip tomorrow?"

"Wait, there's Fruli," Dash said, pointing to the far end of the meadow. "Maybe she can help out."

Fruli spotted the fairies under Dash's mint glow and came over to them. "Is Lyra feeling better?" she asked when she saw the fairies. "I heard from a sugar fly that you brought her to Candy Castle on a sled."

"Yes," Raina said. "She's feeling much better."

"And we just tricked Mogu, so he won't be tracking in salt near the meadow again," Dash told her. "At least, not for a long time."

Fruli smiled. "Oh, I am glad to hear that," she

said. She shuddered. "I've never met Mogu—and I don't want to!"

Raina shrugged. "Oh, he's not that bad," she said. "Just a little salty."

Stepping forward, Raina moved closer to Fruli. "Tomorrow is Berry's birthday," she told her. "We'd like to surprise Berry with a party and also welcome Lyra home. We don't have much time, and we could really use your help."

"How delicious! I would love to help!" Fruli exclaimed. "I didn't know Berry's birthday was on Valentine's Day. I'll have to make her a special heart valentine."

"How about helping with the decorations for the meadow?" Raina asked.

Fruli clapped her hands. "I could do that!" she said. "My aunt just gave me this fabulous

blueberry and cherry material from Meringue Island. We could use it as a tablecloth or something and then get some rainbow lollipops to stick around."

Raina knew she had just asked the right fairy for the job. With Fruli's great design taste, she was sure Fruit Chew Meadow would look *sugar-tacular* by tomorrow's Sun Dip.

"Sure as sugar, this meadow is going to look supersweet," Raina said. "It will be a sugarcoated celebration." She smiled at her friends. "Now we just have to keep the secret from Berry!"

10

A Sugarcoated Day

Raina was up the next morning bright and early. She had so much to do! Not only did she have to feed the animals in Gummy Forest, she had a party to plan!

She'd have to do all her work in the forest quickly and then head to Fruit Chew Meadow. Knowing that she wouldn't have time to fly back home, Raina decided to take her party clothes with her now. Racing around her room, Raina folded her clothes neatly into her backpack. Half of Sugar Valley was coming to Berry and Lyra's surprise party that evening. If everything was going to be finished by Sun Dip, she had to hurry.

Luckily, the gummy animals were well-behaved, and feeding time went well. Thankful that the animals were calm and listening to instructions, Raina gave each one a little extra flavoring. "After all," she told them, "today is a day to celebrate!"

As Raina was cleaning out the gummy bears' feeding log, Melli suddenly appeared before her. The Caramel Fairy's face was bright red, and even when she landed her wings didn't stop fluttering.

"Raina!" Melli gasped. "Oh, I'm so glad I found you here."

Raina dropped the log in the water. "Is Lyra all right?" Raina asked. "What's wrong? Did you hear something?" She eyed her friend's nervous expression.

Melli put her hand up and tried desperately to catch her breath. "Everything is fine," she said. "In fact, everything is more than fine." She smiled. "I'm just bursting to tell you the sweet news!"

"What?" Raina asked. She couldn't imagine what news Melli had for her.

"Guess who is coming to the party tonight?" Melli finally managed to say.

The guest list for the party had gotten so long that Raina had lost count of all the fairies invited. She shook her head. "I don't know," she said, playing along with Melli. "Who?"

"The Sugar Pops!" Melli shouted. Once she said the musical group's name, her wings started flapping again and she soared up to the sky. "Berry is going to flip!"

All the Candy Fairies loved the three brothers who made up the Sugar Pops. Chip, Char, and Carob were three of the most delicious singers. Their music was always at the top of the charts in Sugar Valley.

"That *is* sweet news!" Raina exclaimed. "How do you know? Are you sure?"

The Caramel Fairy nodded quickly. "I was at Candy Castle early this morning to make a delivery, and I saw Princess Lolli," Melli explained. "She told me that Lyra is going home later today and that she'd heard all about the plans for the surprise party." Melli grabbed Raina's hands and started to jump up and down. "And then she told me that Dash had sent a sugar fly to Carob Pop! She let him know about Lyra's being sick, Berry's birthday, and the Valentine's Day celebration. Carob sent her back a sugar fly! Can you believe it?"

Raina shook her head. She was in sugar shock!

"He said he wanted to come sing with Lyra tonight at Sun Dip to help the flowers," Melli continued. She stopped jumping and sank down onto the ground. "Isn't that just the sweetest thing ever?" she swooned.

"Sure as sugar," Raina said.

Melli helped Raina pick up the feeding log and carry it over to the edge of the water. Finally

Melli's wings slowed down, and she was able to breathe normally.

"Having the Sugar Pops sing at the party tonight will sweeten the whole night," Raina said. She grinned at Melli. "Dash found the perfect surprise for Berry."

"And everyone in Sugar Valley!" Melli added.

Raina stuck her hand out and pulled Melli up. "Now we really have to make sure the meadow is looking good," she said. "We're going to have a huge party!"

"I know!" Melli exclaimed. "That's why I had to come here and tell you!"

"And you're sure Berry doesn't know?" Raina asked.

Melli shook her head. "All the sugar flies and fairies know the party is a surprise." Melli grinned. "I have to make sure I don't see Berry today. I don't think I can keep the secret."

Raina rubbed her wet hands on her dress. "I know how you feel," she said. "I'm going to have to avoid Berry all day too! Fruli is going to be with her most of the day and promised to keep her away from the meadow."

"Yes, I heard," Melli said. "And they will escort Lyra back at Sun Dip, right?"

"That's the plan," Raina said. She held up her crossed fingers. "I hope all goes well. I want this to be an extra-special surprise for them both!"

Melli gave Raina a hug. She took off, and called over her shoulder, "I'll see you at Sun Dip!"

Raina stood for a moment, smiling. Their plans were coming together: Lyra was healthy, Berry was going to have a birthday surprise, and now the Sugar Pops were going to sing! This was turning out to be a sugarcoated Valentine's Day.

For Raina, the day was spent making candy for the party and organizing the decorations. She had a quick visit with Lyra at the castle and was happy to see her feeling well.

Back at the meadow, plans for the party were going perfectly. Fruli had dropped off the gorgeous Meringue Island material, and Raina, Cocoa, and Dash hung it as a curtain on the stage.

"For once I'm glad that Berry is always late," Dash said as she hung mint lights around the stage. "I hope we finish in time!"

"Everything looks great," Raina said happily as she took in the scene.

The meadow looked beautiful with the festive decorations, and the flowers were all standing up straight.

"We actually pulled this together!" Dash exclaimed.

"Here they come!" Cocoa shouted. "Places, everyone!"

The fairies all gathered around the stage while the Sugar Pops played. Raina could see the surprised expressions on Berry's and Lyra's faces as they got closer. When the two of them landed on the stage, everyone applauded.

Berry just gazed around the meadow with her mouth open.

"I don't think I've ever seen Berry speechless!" Raina said, giving her friend a tight squeeze. "Happy birthday!"

"I can't think of a sweeter surprise for my birthday *and* Valentine's Day," Berry said. "Thank you all so much." She turned to Raina, Dash, Melli, and Cocoa. "You did all this?"

"Yes," Raina said. "We all helped. Especially Fruli."

Raina handed Berry a present. She was so excited to give Berry her birthday gift. When Raina had visited Lyra earlier that day at Candy Castle, Lyra had told her about the flower she had grown especially for Berry.

"Oh, Raina!" Berry cried. "This is scrumptious!" She put the headband on her head. "I love the fruit-chew flower and all the sparkly gummies."

"I'm glad you like it," Raina said. "Happy birthday, Berry." She went over to Lyra and

stroked her long nose. "And welcome home, Lyra."

Lyra nuzzled Raina's hand. "Thank you," she sang out.

The fairies all exchanged cards and other treats. The whole kingdom was there to celebrate the festive day.

"This turned out to be the sweetest Valentine's Day surprise," Berry said to her friends. "Lyra is healthy, the meadow looks great, and the Sugar Pops are here!"

Raina looked over at Dash and smiled. "Sure as sugar!" she exclaimed happily.

The Sugar Pops played well past when the sun slid behind the Frosted Mountains. Everyone was having a deliciously sweet time.

"This was the best Valentine's Day ever!"

Berry exclaimed at the end of the night.

"And I got some great gifts too," Dash said, grinning.

"Who doesn't love Valentine's Day?" Cocoa added.

Melli and Raina laughed.

"We all got some sweet surprises," Raina said. "But the sweetest part is that we helped Lyra."

"Look at Lyra now," Dash said, smiling.

Lyra was in the meadow, away from the crowds. She was softly singing her special lullaby to the flowers.

"Do you think she liked the party?" Raina asked.

"Yes," Berry said, hugging Raina. "And she loves being back safe and sound, surrounded by all these friends."

Raina smiled. This *was* a grand birthday and Valentine's Day event. There was no better way to celebrate Berry's birthday and Lyra's homecoming. They had tricked Mogu once again, and the Sugar Pops were playing. The sounds coming from the meadow were joyous and sweet. It was a perfect Candy Fairy celebration full of love and friendship!

FIND OUT

WHAT HAPPENS IN

Bubble Gum
Rescue

Early in the morning, Melli the Caramel Fairy flew to the top of Caramel Hills. She was checking on the caramel chocolate rolls she had made with her Chocolate Fairy friend Cocoa. Melli smiled at their newest creation drying in the cool shade of a caramel tree. Yesterday the two fairies had worked hard rolling small logs of caramel and then dipping them in chocolate. The final touch was a drizzle of butterscotch on top. Melli couldn't wait to taste one!

A caramel turtle jutted his head out of his shell and smelled the fresh candy. Melli laughed. "You were hiding over by that log," she said to the turtle. She kneeled down next to him. "Did you think you'd snatch a candy without my noticing?"

The turtle quickly slipped his head back into his shell. Still as a rock, he waited to see what the Caramel Fairy would do.

Melli placed one of the candies in front of him. "Of course you may have one," she said sweetly. "There's enough to share."

The turtle stuck his head out again and gobbled it up.

"Do you like the candy?" Melli asked.

The turtle nodded, and Melli smiled. "Cocoa and I are going to bring these to Sun Dip this evening," she said.

Sun Dip was the time at the end of the day when the sun set behind the Frosted Mountains and the Candy Fairies relaxed. Melli loved visiting with her friends and catching up on everyone's activities. And today she and Cocoa would bring their new candy. She hoped her friends would enjoy the sweet treat.

Just as Melli was putting the candies in her basket, she heard a squeal. It sounded like an animal in trouble. She put the basket down and walked toward the sound.

"Hot caramel!" Melli cried as she peered around one of the caramel trees.

Lying on the ground was a small caramella bird. He was trying to flap his wings to fly, but they were barely moving. Melli leaned in closer and noticed that the bird's feathers were wet and stuck together.

Melli reached out to the bird. "You poor thing," she whispered. She tried to calm the little one by talking to him. Caramella birds lived in the valley of Caramel Hills and had bright yellow wing feathers. They lived off the seeds of the caramel trees and filled the hills with their soft chirps.

"Where have you been playing?" Melli asked sweetly. She carefully picked up the bird and gently stroked his head. Immediately she realized that his feathers were covered in thick butterscotch. "How did you get coated in this syrup?" she asked. "No wonder you can't move or fly."

The bird chirped loudly. It was shaking in her hands.

"Butterscotch is not the best thing for feathers," Melli said, smiling at the tiny caramella. "Don't worry, sweetie," she added softly. "Let's give you a good bath and get this mess off your wings. I know all about sticky caramel." She patted the bird's head gently. "I will get you cleaned up in no time. Let's go to the water well and rinse you off."

Melli held on to the bird and flew to the edge of Caramel Hills. The tiny creature seemed to relax in Melli's hands, but his heart was still pounding. At the well Melli began to wash the butterscotch off the bird's wings. She knew she'd have to spend some time scrubbing. She had gotten caramel on her clothes before, and it often took a while to get all the goo off.

After a few rinses Melli began to see his brightly colored feathers.

"There, that does it," she said, feeling satisfied. She stood back and looked at the little bird. "You do have gorgeous yellow wings!"

The bird shook the water off his wings. He was happy to be able to move them freely. He bowed his head to Melli, thanking her for helping him.

"You should be able to fly now," Melli said. "Be careful, and stay away from the sticky stuff!"

"Hi, Melli!" Cocoa appeared next to her. "What are you doing here?"

"Cocoa," Melli gasped. "You scared me!

I didn't see you there." She pointed to the caramella bird. "Look who I found. He was covered in butterscotch, and his wings were stuck together. I just gave him a bath with the fresh well water."

Cocoa's wings fluttered. "Oh, bittersweet chocolate," she said sadly. "This is worse than I thought."

"What are you talking about?" Melli asked. "He's all clean now. He'll be able to fly."

"It's not only this bird I am worried about," Cocoa said. "I heard from a sugar fly that there was a butterscotch syrup spill on the eastern side of Butterscotch Volcano. That must be where this one got syrup on his wings. *All* the caramella birds are in danger!"

"Oh no," Melli said. "So many caramella birds

live over there. What else did the sugar fly tell you?"

"That was all," Cocoa replied.

Sugar flies passed information around Sugar Valley. If a fairy wanted to get the word out about something important, the sugar flies were the ones to spread the news. "Let's go now," Melli said urgently. "If Butterscotch Volcano erupts, there'll be a large spill in the hills." She looked down at the bird. "Is that what happened to you? Will you take us to where you got butterscotch on your wings?"

The bird took flight, and Melli and Cocoa trailed after him. His yellow feathers gleamed in the sunlight. Melli beat her wings faster. She was very concerned about what kind of sticky mess they were going to find.

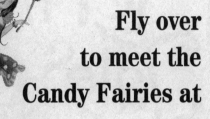

Fly over
to meet the
Candy Fairies at

CandyFairies.com

See what the Fairies left behind:

- A sweet eCard to send to your friends
- *Choc-o-rific* activities
- Delicious recipes

All you need to know about your favorite characters!

The
Sugar Ball

Candy Fairies

The Sugar Ball

HELEN PERELMAN

ILLUSTRATED BY
ERICA-JANE WATERS

ALADDIN
NEW YORK   LONDON   TORONTO   SYDNEY

ALADDIN

An imprint of Simon & Schuster Children's Publishing Division

1230 Avenue of the Americas, New York, NY 10020

First Aladdin paperback edition October 2011

Text copyright © 2011 by Helen Perelman Bernstein

Illustrations copyright © 2011 by Erica-Jane Waters

All rights reserved, including the right of reproduction in whole or in part in any form.

ALADDIN is a trademark of Simon & Schuster, Inc., and related logo is a registered
trademark of Simon & Schuster, Inc.

For information about special discounts for bulk purchases, please contact
Simon & Schuster Special Sales at 1-866-506-1949 or business@simonandschuster.com.

The Simon & Schuster Speakers Bureau can bring authors to your live event.
For more information or to book an event contact the Simon & Schuster Speakers
Bureau at 1-866-248-3049 or visit our website at www.simonspeakers.com.

Designed by Karin Paprocki

The text of this book was set in Berthold Baskerville Book.

Manufactured in the United States of America 0814 OFF

4 6 8 10 9 7 5

Library of Congress Control Number 2011932360

ISBN 978-1-4424-0825-8

ISBN 978-1-4424-0826-5 (eBook)

For Karli and Hana Grace Meyer

Contents

The Sugar Ball

1

Sweet Thoughts

Cocoa smiled as she flew across Chocolate Woods. The sun was shining and the air was full of sweet, rich chocolate scents. The Chocolate Fairy spread her golden wings and glided down to Chocolate Falls. *Yum*, thought Cocoa as she licked her lips. There was nothing better than fresh milk chocolate.

"Cocoa!" Melli the Caramel Fairy called. "Over here!" Melli was sitting underneath a chocolate oak tree. She waved to get Cocoa's attention.

Waving back, Cocoa fluttered down to her friend's side. Melli was always on time—or early. She was a shy fairy, but her sweet caramel nature was part of what kept their group of friends sticking together—no matter what.

"What a *choc-o-rific* day!" Cocoa sang. She smiled at her friend.

"Only one more week until the Sugar Ball," Melli burst out. "I can't wait!" She took out a light caramel twist from her bag. "What do you think? I just had to show you right away." She held up the long caramel rope candy for Cocoa to view.

"It looks delicious," Cocoa commented.

"Won't this be perfect for the sash on my dress?" Melli asked. "I've been searching for just the right size trim."

Cocoa laughed. All any of her friends could think about was the Sugar Ball at Candy Castle and the dresses they'd wear to the party. The big ball was the grandest—and sweetest—of the season. The Sugar Ball was a celebration of the sugar harvest. Fairies from all over came to the Royal Gardens for the party. Princess Lolli, the ruling fairy princess, always made the party the most scrumptious of the year.

"I think that will be the perfect addition to your outfit," Cocoa said. She touched the golden caramel twist. "This is the exact right color for your dress."

 3

Melli clapped her hands. "I knew you'd say that!" she said, grinning. "Cara wanted me to make her one just like this too."

Cara was Melli's little sister and always wanted to be just like her big sister.

"Did you help her?" Cocoa asked.

"Sure as sugar," Melli said. "She's so excited about her first ball." She stopped and admired her dress. "Now I just need to find the right necklace."

"You should ask Berry to make you one of her sparkly fruit-chew necklaces," Cocoa said. She was used to her friend Berry the Fruit Fairy always talking about fashion, but this year all her friends were concerned about their Sugar Ball dresses and jewelry. Everyone wanted to make her ball gown special and unique. Even Cocoa!

"You're right," Melli said. "I should ask Berry. I just hope she doesn't say she's too busy. Did you know that she is weaving the material for her dress herself? Her dress is going to be *sweet-tacular*!"

"Hmm," Cocoa muttered. She was actually growing a little tired of all the talk about dresses. Even though she wanted to look her best, she had another idea of how to make her entrance at the ball special.

"Do you think Char will remember me?" Melli asked, interrupting Cocoa's thoughts. Her light brown eyes had a faraway gaze. Like most fairies in Sugar Valley, she loved the Sugar Pops. They were brothers who played in a band together and sang the sweetest songs. Char was the lead singer in the band and Melli's supersweet crush.

"How could they forget you?" Cocoa asked. "You were the Candy Fairy who saved Caramel Moon!" In the fall, when the candy corn crop was in danger, Melli was the one who discovered the problem. Together with their fairy friends, they saved the Caramel Moon festival, where the Sugar Pops played. They even got to meet Carob, Chip, and Char! Seeing them again at the Sugar Ball would definitely sugarcoat the night.

"I know it's just a rumor that they'll come," Melli said, "but I hope the sugar fly buzz is right. I would love to see them again." Melli clasped her hands together and put them under her chin. She looked over at Cocoa. "What's in your bag?"

Looking down at her bag, Cocoa smiled. There were a couple of strands of marshmallow threads sticking out of her chocolate weave bag. "I was down at Marshmallow Marsh this morning," she explained.

"What are you doing with marshmallow?" Melli asked. "You can't use that for your dress. Marshmallow is too sticky to work for an outfit."

Cocoa laughed. "No, not for my dress," she said. "Something else for the ball." She sat down and took out a sheet of paper from her pocket. "Last week when Raina was reading from the Fairy Code Book, there was that story about the princess and her chocolate scepter. Do you remember?"

Raina the Gummy Fairy was their good friend, who loved to read. She had nearly memorized the entire Fairy Code Book!

Nodding, Melli thought back to the story. "It was a magic scepter made of the finest sugar. The picture in the book showed a beautiful chocolate wand."

"Yes," Cocoa said, "and I was thinking that I'd like to make a chocolate scepter for the ball. Wouldn't that be so sweet, to walk in holding a royal scepter?" Cocoa sighed. "I'd be like a fairy princess!"

Just thinking about the scepter made Cocoa's wings flutter. Even though she was excited about her new strawberry-and-chocolate dot dress with a purple candy butterfly, she couldn't wait to hold a royal scepter. "It will be like a magic wand!"

"You will look like a fairy princess," Melli agreed. Then she paused. "Do you know how to make a magic wand?"

Cocoa shook her head. "No, but I plan on learning. I made a sketch of the scepter that I'd like to make." She held up her drawing. "Did you bring me the caramel ball mold? I wanted

to have a round chocolate sphere at the top."

Melli pulled the round mold out of her bag and gave it to Cocoa. "I was wondering what you were going to do with this," she said.

"I'm meeting Raina later," Cocoa told her. "She's going to lend me a book about magic wands." Carefully, Cocoa folded her drawing up and put the paper back in her bag. "I thought the marshmallow would add a nice touch."

"I think you're right." Melli nodded.

"And I'll need lots of this chocolate," Cocoa added. She took out a pail and dipped it into the pool of chocolate swirling in front of her. "The waterfall chocolate is the best for making special chocolate candies. I need to hurry home so the chocolate can set. Then I'm going to carve decorations on the ball."

"I can't wait to see that chocolate wand!" Melli cried.

"Thanks," Cocoa replied. She swept up her bucket and headed back to Chocolate Woods. She had lots of work to do before Sun Dip tonight. A chocolate magic wand was no small task. And Cocoa wanted to make sure it was going to be the talk of the Sugar Ball.

2

The Chocolate Scepter

When Cocoa returned to Chocolate Woods, she poured the fresh chocolate into Melli's hard caramel mold. She knew that she wanted a chocolate ball at the top of her wand—just like the one she had seen in Raina's book. Later, when the chocolate was hard, she would carefully carve the ball with her tools. Oh, she couldn't wait! Her magic scepter was going to be *choc-o-rific*!

While the chocolate was hardening, Cocoa flew to Gummy Forest to find Raina. Her friend had not one, as promised, but two books on magic wands.

"You should know that it's often sticky business to make magic wands," Raina told her. She pushed her long hair out of her eyes as she spoke. "If wands get into the wrong hands, there can be trouble."

Cocoa laughed. "Oh, chocolate sticks," she said. "It's just for my costume. Raina, you worry too much. And I don't think I am going to let go of it. I've been working so hard on the wand. I'll want to hold my perfect accessory all evening!"

Raina handed the two large books to Cocoa.

"Here you go," she said. "These are two books that have a few different pictures of royal scepters."

Flipping through the pages, Cocoa's eyes grew wide with excitement. "Oh, this is perfect!" she exclaimed. She noticed the details in the chocolate carvings and the bright colors used for the wands. She had so many ideas, and she wanted to get started right away.

Cocoa felt a gentle nudge and looked down. "Hi, Nokie," she said. Nokie was a little red gummy bear cub. He was always hungry. Even though he didn't eat chocolate, he was hoping that Cocoa might have a treat for him. "I have some fruit chews, if you want," she told him. "Berry gave them to me yesterday, and I'm not going to use them for my hair clips."

Nokie eagerly nodded. Berry had given him fruit chews before and he loved the fruity, sparkly candy.

"Nokie!" Raina scolded. But she couldn't help smiling at the cute cub when she saw his face. Her voice softened. "Just one, okay?"

The gummy cub quickly agreed and took Cocoa's offering.

"Sorry about that," Raina apologized to Cocoa. "No matter how much I feed Nokie, he's always hungry!"

Cocoa patted the friendly cub on his belly. "It's okay," she said. "I'm happy to share."

"Do you want to see my dress?" Raina asked. "The color came out perfectly!" She showed her friend the bright lime-green dress with rainbow gummy accents on the waist and hem. She held the gown up to show off the details.

"Oh, Raina," Cocoa gasped. "This is really beautiful. You made this by yourself?"

Raina blushed. "Well, I had some help from Berry. She's so good at designing and sewing. I'm not sure what I would have done without her."

"You are going to look delicious," Cocoa told her. "Have you decided how you'll wear your hair?"

Raina shrugged. "I'm not sure yet," she confided. "Maybe I'll get a fancy updo. What do you think?" She pulled her long, straight hair up and twisted it in a fancy bun. "I could use a rainbow gummy berry for a clip."

"I can't wait to see what you decide," Cocoa told her. "Sure as sugar, every fairy in Sugar

Valley is going to look extra-sweet."

"I know!" Raina exclaimed. "I can't wait!"

Cocoa glanced over at the Frosted Mountains. "I better get going," she said. "I want to carve the chocolate ball before Sun Dip tonight." She winked at Raina. "Maybe I'll bring the wand for a special preview."

"Oh, please do!" Raina pleaded. "I'd love to see what you do." She took Nokie's paw and gave a wave to her friend. "I've got to take Nokie back to his den. I'll see you later."

"Thanks for the books," Cocoa called. She took off and flew swiftly back to Chocolate Woods.

At home Cocoa saw the chocolate in her mold was hard and dry. She selected the smallest pink sugar crystal carving tool for the delicate design of the chocolate wand. The tiny tool was good for small details. She glanced over at one of the books Raina had given her. She was looking at a couple of different wands and using ideas that she loved about each one. Skillfully she carved a beautiful design on the chocolate ball.

When she finished she stood back and gazed at her sphere. She placed the ball on top of the wand using very hot chocolate and sugar. Then she added a few glittering candy jewels that she had been saving for a special occasion and a bit of white marshmallow as a finishing touch.

She pointed the wand at a cracker on the table, and instantly it was covered in chocolate.

"Hot chocolate!" she exclaimed. "I really did it!"

The lavender light seeping through her window alerted her to the time. Her friends were probably already gathered for Sun Dip. She took her wand, eager for her friends to see her handiwork.

As she had suspected all her friends were together near the shores of Red Licorice Lake for Sun Dip. Even Berry was there! Berry was hardly ever on time, but she must have been very excited to show off her new fruit-chew jewelry and her ball gown.

"Did you finish your wand?" Melli called out as soon as she spotted Cocoa.

Cocoa proudly took her prized possession out of her bag. She floated above her friends and waved her royal scepter. Tiny little pieces of chocolate sprinkled from the wand, and her friends giggled as they grabbed for the sweets.

"*So mint!*" Dash called out. The little Mint Fairy was the smallest fairy in Sugar Valley, but also one of the fastest. She swooped through the air to gather up the most chocolate. "Cocoa, your wand is beautiful—and *choc-o-rific*!"

"You certainly have a way with chocolate," Melli said.

"Thanks," Cocoa said, grinning. "I can't wait for the ball. We're going to have the best time!"

"And wait till the Sugar Pops see us!" Melli gushed.

"They won't even recognize us," Berry boasted. "The last time we saw them, we weren't in ball gowns. We'd been working in Candy Corn Fields!" She slipped her long gown on over her dress. "Cocoa, will you zip me up?"

"Sure," Cocoa said, setting down the wand. "This gown is *sweet-tacular*!"

Berry twirled around in a circle. The meringue bottom of her dress fell around her in a puffed-out skirt. "I feel like a princess!" she said, beaming.

"And you look like one too," Raina told her. "I think we all will tomorrow night!"

"I better get back home," Cocoa said. She looked up at the sky. The sun was almost behind the Frosted Mountains. "I have to finish my dress." She grabbed her royal wand and put it in her bag. "I'll see you fairies tomorrow!" she cried as she shot up in the air. "I can't wait for the Sugar Ball!"

CHAPTER 3

Chocolate Clues

Speeding through Sugar Valley, Cocoa was grinning as she thought about the Sugar Ball. She wondered what Princess Lolli would say about her wand; after all, she was a *real* fairy princess. The ruling princess of Candy Kingdom certainly knew all about royal wands. Cocoa had long admired the fancy bejeweled candy scepter that Princess Lolli held at important affairs. Her great-grandmother Queen Taffy had passed down the wand to her. It was beautiful and sparkled with the most exquisite rainbow sugar candies. Cocoa hoped Princess Lolli would be pleased with her chocolate one!

When she arrived home, she put her bag on the chocolate oak table and examined her unfinished dress. She wanted to put a few extra chocolate sprinkles on the waistband.

As she sewed, Cocoa thought about the ball. Sugar Ball was known for elaborate candies made specially by the Royal Fairies at Candy Castle. Everything at the ball was sugarcoated and delicious! Holding a wand all night might be difficult. If she were to eat any candy, she'd need a free hand. Maybe if she sewed a loop on the side of the dress, she could easily slip the wand in and out.

Cocoa was very pleased with herself. What a *choc-o-rific* idea! She cut some extra fabric and got to work.

The stars twinkled in the dark night sky, and the full moon cast a white glow through Cocoa's window. She'd been hard at work for hours! Cocoa stood back and examined her finished gown. She was so proud of her dress— and the fancy loop on the side of the dress for the wand. Grabbing her chocolate weave bag from the table, she reached inside for her wand to test out her invention.

"Huh?" Cocoa murmured to herself. She stuck her hand into her bag. Where was the wand?

She knew she had put the wand back into her bag before leaving Sun Dip. She never would have left the wand lying on the ground. . . .

She searched the bag again. And then she saw her finger poking through a hole at the bottom of her bag. A hole that was big enough for her chocolate wand to fall through!

"Bittersweet chocolate!" she cried.

Cocoa's heart began to race. Her magic wand was gone? Raina's words rang in Cocoa's head. *If wands get into the wrong hands, there can be trouble.*

The first sour thought that came into Cocoa's head was of the salty old troll Mogu. Mogu lived under the bridge in Black Licorice Swamp and was always on the hunt for Candy Fairy candy. He had even stolen Cocoa's prized chocolate eggs from their nest in Chocolate

Woods. Cocoa's wings fluttered as she remembered her journey to Black Licorice Swamp with Princess Lolli. The princess had been brave as well as clever, and together, the two fairies had outsmarted that old troll. Would he have tried to steal from her again?

Cocoa rushed outside and called for the sugar flies. She had to get messages to her friends quickly. Sugar flies could be gossips, but they were also good for getting messages to friends in a hurry.

Dashing off notes to her friends, Cocoa instructed the flies to deliver the urgent messages. Cocoa knew it was late, but she asked her friends to meet her back at Red Licorice Lake. Since that was the last time she'd seen the wand, she figured she would begin her search there.

After the sugar flies took flight, Cocoa flew to the Sun Dip meeting spot. She hoped that on her way she'd spot the wand. Even though the moonlight was bright, Cocoa didn't see any candy jewels glittering on the ground. All that hard work—and all that chocolate magic! Cocoa was melting inside. How could she have been so careless? She should have double-checked her bag!

At Red Licorice Lake, Cocoa took a peppermint light from her pocket. She held the candy up as she searched the red sugar sand beach.

Not a trace of her wand.

Cocoa sat down on the cool red sugar sand. The valley was dark, and most fairies were home getting ready for bed. Her wings drooped as she thought about having to tell Princess

Lolli her wand had been lost. A magic wand gone missing was not something to take lightly. She'd have to tell her. If Mogu had gotten hold of the wand, there was no telling what would happen! The Sugar Ball would be canceled. All of Sugar Valley would be in danger. A troll with a magic wand . . . She didn't even want to think about it.

Cocoa pulled her knees up to her chest and buried her head. She hoped that the sugar flies had delivered her messages quickly and that her friends would come soon. Maybe together they'd be able to figure out what to do.

Glancing up, Cocoa saw a thick licorice stalk in front of her. She squinted in the moonlight, unsure of what she was looking at. What was on the top of the stalk? She stood up and flew to the top of the licorice.

It was covered in chocolate syrup!

Someone definitely found the wand here, Cocoa thought. The wand must have fallen out as soon as she took flight! Flying around the stalk, Cocoa wondered why someone would have aimed at the licorice stalk. She floated back down to the ground, searching for more clues. If she followed the chocolate clues, she'd find the wand!

She wasn't sure her plan would work, but she knew one thing. Sure as sugar, she needed all her friends to help her!

CHAPTER 4

Spreading Chocolate

Cocoa!" Melli cried. She swooped down and knelt near her friend. "Oh, Cocoa, what is going on?" She took a deep breath. "I saw chocolate puddles everywhere as I flew from Caramel Hills!"

Looking up at her friend, Cocoa's lip quivered. She didn't want to burst into tears, so she looked back down at her knees. "My wand . . . ," she began.

Melli's hand was on her back. "Oh, Cocoa. You worked so hard on that wand." And then she took a quick breath as she realized what this news meant. "And now someone has chocolate power!" she gasped.

"Licking lollipops!" Berry blurted out when she saw her friends. "What is going on here tonight? There's a chocolate explosion around here. You should see Fruit Chew Meadow! Those candy chews are going to need a power wash to get back to their fruity glory."

"There's chocolate in Fruit Chew Meadow, too?" Cocoa asked. She shook her head. This was worse than she had thought. Someone was definitely using the wand—someone who didn't understand the magic of chocolate.

"Strange," Berry said. She tapped her finger to her chin. "It's like there's a chocolate spell on Sugar Valley or something."

"And that spell is *so mint*!" Dash announced as she flew in from over the licorice stalks. "These peppermints are delicious with the chocolate sprayed on them. What a minty cool idea." She popped a chocolate-covered candy in her mouth and then licked her fingers.

"Dash!" Melli scolded. "This isn't a joke. Cocoa's magic wand has been stolen!"

"Not stolen, exactly," Cocoa said sadly. "My wand fell out of my bag when I left Sun Dip." She couldn't keep back her tears anymore. "And now this is all my fault! Raina warned me about making a magic wand."

Cocoa's friends all gasped. A gentle breeze blew and fluttered their wings as the fairies stood in silence.

"Oh, this doesn't look good," Raina said as she joined her friends. She looked at Cocoa. "I came as soon as I got the message. What happened?"

"Please tell me you know a story in the Fairy Code Book about a magic wand that gets into the wrong hands," Cocoa pleaded. She held up her bag and stuck her fingers in the hole. "My wand fell out after I left Sun Dip."

"Hot caramel," Melli muttered. "This is really a sticky situation." Then she realized why Cocoa was so upset. "Do you think Mogu could have picked up the wand?"

"Mogu can't make chocolate," Berry argued. "He's a troll."

"No, but if he is holding a magic wand that was made by a chocolate fairy," Raina said, thinking out loud, "then it might be possible."

Cocoa jumped up from the ground. "What do you mean, *might be possible?*" She grabbed Raina's hand. "You mean in all the stories you've ever read, you've never come across this?" She hung her head. "Oh, this is really bad."

Raina paced back and forth on the red sugar sand. "I don't know," she said. "I'm thinking."

The fairies all watched Raina. They weren't used to seeing her flustered. Raina was always so sure and logical. And usually she could quote a line from the Fairy Code Book that would solve their problem.

"But Raina always knows the answer!" Dash blurted out.

Berry and Melli shot her a look, but Dash just shrugged.

"Raina said it *might* be possible," Berry said. "Maybe there's hope that Mogu couldn't make this chocolate mess."

"That's a chance we can't take," Cocoa said. She stood up. "We need to follow the chocolate trail. Tracking the clues is the only way to find the wand."

Raina nodded. "Cocoa's right. Let's try to figure out where the wand is . . ."

"And who has it," Berry finished for her.

"What if Mogu did take the wand?" Melli asked. She shivered as she thought of the old troll having chocolate power. "What a gooey mess we're in! And right before the Sugar Ball."

"It's my mess," Cocoa said. "I'm going to fly

north toward Candy Castle. From your reports, the chocolate seems to be spreading in that direction."

"You are not going alone," Melli said, standing next to her.

"Sure as sugar, we're all going with you," Raina added.

Dash and Berry nodded. And they all leaned in to hug Cocoa.

"Thank you," Cocoa managed to say. "This means so much to me. I can't bear the thought of facing Princess Lolli with another chocolate mess."

"Don't get your wings stuck in syrup yet," Berry teased. "We can solve this mystery."

Together, the fairies flew to Candy Castle. The pink-and-white sugarcoated castle glistened in the moonlight. The frosted towers and iced tips of the castle looked the same as always. She sighed, relieved that there wasn't a blanket of chocolate covering the castle or the Royal Gardens.

"Doesn't look like there is any chocolate out of place here," Cocoa said.

"Look over there," Raina whispered, pointing. "It's Tula, Princess Lolli's adviser. I wonder what she's doing in the gardens so late at night."

"She's talking to a bunch of Sour Orchard Fairies," Berry said. Berry had once been scared to go to Sour Orchard. She had to find Lemona the Sour Orchard Fairy, who had created the heart-shaped candies Berry found by Chocolate River. After Berry met her, she found out that those fairies weren't so different from Berry and her friends. Berry squinted her eyes. "I think that might even be Lemona!"

Just then Tula flew into the castle, and Lemona was left standing in the gardens.

"I'm going to ask her what's going on," Berry said. Before Cocoa or the others could react, Berry was at Lemona's side. And then in a flash, Berry was back with news.

"Lemona said that the Sour Orchard was covered in chocolate syrup. Princess Lolli is very concerned about the chocolate mess. She said she'll cancel the Sugar Ball! There can't be a royal celebration when so many parts of the kingdom are under a chocolate spell."

"Oh, this means we're in hot chocolate," Cocoa mumbled. She twisted a strand of her long, dark hair around her finger.

"We need to break this spell immediately!" Berry shouted.

"But first we need to find out who has the wand," Cocoa added quietly.

CHAPTER

5

Chocolate Bash

The place Cocoa wanted to check first was Gummy Forest. Raina hadn't seen any chocolate in the forest before she got Cocoa's message, so maybe that was the next place for a chocolate attack. If Cocoa and her friends followed the chocolate, they'd find the wand. And right now Cocoa knew they had to find that wand before all of Sugar Valley was put under a thick, gooey spell!

The moonlight made Gummy Forest look different. Even though Cocoa had been there many times, in the dark the gummy trees and bushes took on spooky shapes. There were chocolate puddles along the ground, and random flowers and berries were chocolate-covered.

Whoever had the wand didn't really know how to handle it—or the magic. The syrupy chocolate was aimed all over the place, and not with a real purpose, the way a Chocolate Fairy would use the wand. Cocoa sighed as she flew through the trees hoping to find her next clue. She had never seen Gummy Forest in such a state. Looking over at Raina, she saw her Gummy Fairy friend was trying to be brave.

"Once we find the wand, I promise to help clean up this mess," Cocoa told Raina. "I am so sorry."

Raina glanced over at Cocoa as they flew. "It's not your fault," Raina said. "The wand falling out of your bag was an accident."

Cocoa lowered her head. She still felt responsible for the chocolate mess.

And then she saw something that made her heart stop.

In a hammock between two large gummy trees, Cocoa spotted Mogu. She froze and put her hand up to alert her friends. The five fairies huddled in the air just above the troll. Mogu was just as Cocoa had remembered him: lying down stuffing his mouth full of chocolate. His hands and face were stained with dark splotches of chocolate, and his large nose was sniffing a chocolate-covered gummy flower. He was making loud slurping sounds as he ate all the chocolate around him.

Cocoa took a deep breath. She tried to summon all the courage that she could. After watching Princess Lolli in Black Licorice Swamp, she knew she had to be brave as well as clever to trick this hungry old troll. She motioned for her friends to stay where they were, and she got ready to fly down to face Mogu.

Melli grabbed her hand. "Do you want me to go with you?" she asked.

Cocoa shook her head. "No, I need to do this

 47

alone. It's my chocolate wand, and I'm going to get it back."

Her friends all exchanged looks, but they knew that when Cocoa got stuck on an idea, that was the end of the discussion.

"I'll be fine," she said. "I've talked to Mogu before. This time, I know what I need to do. Besides, I know you are right behind me."

"Sure as sugar," Melli said, smiling.

Cocoa flew down to the hammock and took a deep breath.

"Mogu," Cocoa said as she landed next to him. She was surprised at how calm and sure she sounded.

"Ah, the little Chocolate Fairy!" Mogu said. *"Bah-haaaaa,"* he laughed. "I see you have been busy. I love what you've added to this place. I always thought this forest needed a little more chocolate."

Mogu's ring of white hair around his head was sticking up. And his dark, beady eyes were wide with greed. Cocoa tried to steady her breath. She felt as if there was a fire in her belly, heating her up.

Be calm, she thought.

"What are you doing here?" Cocoa asked.

"I'm having an old chocolate bash," Mogu laughed. "What does it look like I'm doing? These chocolate-covered gummy berries are pretty, pretty good." He licked his fingers. *"Bah-ha-ha-haaaaaaa!"*

Cocoa stared at Mogu. He seemed to be on the verge of eating too much chocolate. He didn't look scary. His stomach looked too full of chocolate to allow him to get up. And he had that crazed chocolate gaze in his eyes that she remembered from when she and Princess Lolli had gone to Black Licorice Swamp. He was close to going into a chocolate slumber. Cocoa hoped that wasn't too far off. Then she could search for the wand without his noticing.

"I never would have thought to cover these candies in chocolate!" Mogu said with a loud burp. He reached his hand down and scooped up a bunch more berries.

Cocoa shot her friends a look. Maybe Mogu was *eating* the chocolate, not *making* the chocolate. She scanned the area and didn't see the wand anywhere. Suddenly Cocoa was encouraged. A lost wand was one thing, but it was another thing if a sour troll had it. And the only thing Mogu seemed to have was a chocolate appetite!

"Maybe you'd like some more chocolate?" Cocoa asked.

She could tell her friends were confused by her offer, but Cocoa suddenly felt very confident.

"Bah-ha-haaaaaaaa!" Mogu laughed. "I would love that!"

"Well, if you had a magic wand, you could make your own chocolate," Cocoa said. She watched Mogu's face carefully. "You wouldn't need a fairy to make the candy for you."

Mogu stopped eating and stared at Cocoa. "What a big idea from such a small fairy," Mogu muttered. "I want one of those!"

"I bet you would," Cocoa said, smiling. She was so relieved that Mogu didn't have the wand that she touched a gummy flower and gave the

candy a rich, dark chocolate shell with chocolate sprinkles. "Here," she said. She handed the greedy troll the special treat. "Try this."

Mogu ate the candy as Cocoa flew up to her friends. "Mogu doesn't have the wand!" she exclaimed.

"Why'd you give him more candy?" Dash blurted out.

"Because the faster Mogu falls asleep, the sooner he'll stop eating all of Gummy Forest!" Cocoa said, winking at Dash.

"And we've got work to do. We can't spend all day troll-sitting!" Raina said.

Cocoa was thankful to have her friends around her. Together, they would find a way to stop this chocolate spell from spreading all over Sugar Valley.

CHAPTER 6

Chocolate Storm

The five fairies watched Mogu sleeping. His mouth fell open, and he began snoring loudly. His chocolate-covered hands dangled off the hammock. With each breath he took, his big belly went up and down. Cocoa was right. The greedy troll's chocolate slumber had begun.

"Now Mogu won't eat all of Gummy Forest!"

Raina declared happily. She sent a sugar fly to Candy Castle with news of Mogu's appearance in the forest. The Royal Fairy Guards would safely fly the sleeping Mogu back to Black Licorice Swamp. The troll would not be eating any more of the Candy Fairies' candy for a while.

Meanwhile the five friends flew back to Raina's home. They needed a place to think and figure out what to do next.

"Before we start following clues all over Sugar Valley, we need to figure out a plan," Berry said.

Cocoa knew her levelheaded friend was right, but she was anxious to get out and see if there were more chocolate clues. She couldn't help but feel this chocolate mess was all her fault. The faster she found the wand, the faster this would all be over.

"Raina, maybe we should see if anything like this has ever happened in Sugar Valley before," Melli said. "I know you said that you couldn't remember anything in the Fairy Code Book, but maybe we can help you look." She glanced over at the wall of books in Raina's room.

"I'm thinking," Raina replied. She was staring at her large bookcase. "There might be something in one of these books." She flew up to the top shelf and then glided back down with three yellow books in her hands. "I remember some kind of chocolate storm. It's barely mentioned in the Fairy Code Book, but maybe the story is in here."

"Why isn't the story in the Fairy Code Book?" Dash asked, peering over her shoulder.

Raina shrugged. "Sometimes there is more to a story than the Fairy Code Book records," she

said. She opened up one of the yellow books. Dust flew from the covers. "Sweet sugar!" she said, blowing away the dust. "I guess I haven't opened this in a while!"

"Are these stories all true?" Cocoa asked.

"I believe that they are," Raina said. "And I think I just found the chocolate storm story!"

Cocoa raced forward to sit next to Raina. All the fairies huddled around as Raina began to tell the story. The way Raina read the story, it felt as if they were all there.

"The sky was filled with dark clouds, and all the fairies in Sugar Valley knew that a winter storm was coming," Raina read. "All the sugar flies were buzzing with the news of terrible weather. Fairies snuggled inside and prepared for the winter storm."

"Yum. I bet they were all drinking hot chocolate with marshmallows!" Dash blurted out. "And the slopes on the Frosted Mountains must have been *so mint*!"

Cocoa smiled at Dash. Even at a time like this, Dash was happy to think about sweets and sledding.

"The snow that fell that day was different from other winter storms," Raina continued to read. "The normal winter white snow that usually fell in Sugar Valley didn't come. Instead, the snow was a deep, brown chocolate powder and piled up in high drifts around the valley."

"So they could just make hot chocolate by sticking their cups in the snow!" Dash interrupted.

"Shhh," Melli scolded gently. "Let Raina finish."

Raina looked over at Dash and winked. Then she read more. "The storm lasted for a week. No one knew what to make of the weather. But the fluffy sweet powder was nothing that anyone had ever seen before."

Cocoa leaned over to the book and read the next line with a heavy heart. "Some said it was a gift," she read. "And others said it was a curse. Sugar Valley was under a chocolate spell."

"So mint," Dash said. "I would have had plenty to make out of chocolate snow! Peppermint and chocolate is delicious!"

"The chocolate snow stayed around for weeks," Raina read, turning the page. "Many fairies were cooped up inside their homes. Most fairies learned how to make all sorts of chocolate treats using the powdered chocolate. They had to use the snow. There was so much chocolate!"

"What happened?" Berry asked.

Melli inched forward. She bit her nails. "Go on, Raina," she said. "Tell us what happened."

"The chocolate snow started to melt," Raina said. "There were great chocolate floods, and Chocolate River overflowed."

"What a chocolate mess!" Melli muttered.

Raina nodded and continued to read. "The snow seeped into all the sugar soil."

"Oh no," Melli said. "The crops!" Her hand flew to her mouth.

"The spring and summer crops all had a hint of chocolate," Raina read. "It took two whole years to rid the soil of the chocolate taste."

"Bittersweet," Cocoa said, shaking her head. "Too much chocolate is never a good idea."

Berry stood up and walked around. "Do you think the chocolate syrup puddles we saw are going to ruin the candy crops?"

Melli shot Berry a look.

"What?" Berry said. "I'm just asking."

Cocoa lowered her head. "Berry is asking a good question," she said. She knew that Melli didn't like it when the friends didn't get along, but Cocoa couldn't be mad at Berry for stating the truth. The crops were in danger. This situation was more serious than the Sugar Ball being canceled. They had to fix this problem quickly before the chocolate spread all over Sugar Valley.

Raina closed the book.

Cocoa sighed. Now what were they going to do?

7

Chocolate Thoughts

Cocoa fiddled with her chocolate dot bracelet. No one said a word after Raina finished reading the story of the great chocolate storm. Cocoa lifted her eyes from her wrist and glanced at her four friends. Their worried expressions made Cocoa uneasy. The missing chocolate wand could ruin all the candy in Sugar Valley.

At that moment she almost wished that Mogu had stolen the magic chocolate wand. At least she had some idea how to handle the salty old troll. But now she felt helpless.

Just then Cocoa felt Melli's arm around her. "We need to find the wand, that's all," she said quietly.

"Melli's right," Berry chimed in. "This isn't a huge chocolate snowstorm. Chances are, these chocolate puddles will dry up quickly. The candy crops will be fine."

"We don't know that," Cocoa whispered.

"Let's see what we do know," Raina said. She took out a notebook and started writing. "There's a missing magic chocolate wand. And chocolate from Sour Orchard all the way to Gummy Forest."

"Someone has definitely gotten hold of the wand. Someone who is clearly not a Chocolate Fairy," Dash said.

Melli flew over to Dash and gave her a tight squeeze. "That's it!" she shouted. "What we need is a Chocolate Fairy to make another wand to clean up the mess! A new magic wand could get rid of the chocolate spell."

"She'd need the first wand to be able to reverse the spell," Raina said, shaking her head.

"But maybe I could make something to help clean up the mess," Cocoa blurted out. "I just can't sit here wondering what to do." She stood up. "Send a sugar fly if you hear or see anything," Cocoa told them. "I'm going back to Chocolate Woods."

"Do you want company?" Melli asked.

Cocoa fluttered her wings. "Maybe in a little while," she said. "For now I need to concentrate on chocolate thoughts."

As Cocoa headed back to Chocolate Woods, she was saddened to see all the puddles of chocolate in Sugar Valley. Berry was right . . . whoever had the wand was not a Chocolate Fairy. A Chocolate Fairy would know how to hold the wand with better aim and skill. She shook her head. But what Candy Fairy would want to steal her wand?

Before Cocoa went into Chocolate Woods, she decided to sit on Caramel Hills to think. She was happy to see that there was no sign of chocolate on the golden hill.

Cocoa sat and wondered what would happen to the crops and thought about how sad all the fairies would be if there was no Sugar Ball. A tear fell from Cocoa's eye. How could she even tell Princess Lolli? To think that she had once been so excited about her chocolate royal wand!

Out of the corner of her eye, Cocoa saw a flash of chocolate. At first she thought she was seeing things. But then she realized—there was a chocolate clue happening right in front of her!

She got up and flew toward the caramel tree dripping with chocolate. She touched the chocolate. The thin chocolate was like syrup.

How strange, she thought. *The wand must be nearby.*

She flew up to the top of the tree and looked around. This had to be a fresh hit. The chocolate hadn't been there before. Her wings began to flutter. Was this the final chocolate clue? She scooted to the edge of the tree branch and scouted the area. She didn't realize it, but she was holding her breath. She was nervous and excited at the same time. Right beside a small chocolate oak tree she spotted her chocolate royal wand!

The sight took her breath away, and she gasped out loud. Cocoa saw the wand—and knew the fairy holding it!

8

The Power of Chocolate

Cocoa flew down to the small chocolate oak. Her eyes never left her chocolate wand. "Cara, what are you doing with that?" she asked the small Caramel Fairy. Melli's little sister stood wide-eyed, staring back at her.

"Oh, Cocoa!" Cara cried. Tears sprang from her eyes and she sobbed so hard that Cocoa couldn't understand a word she was saying.

At that moment Cocoa wasn't angry at all. She reached out, took the wand, and put her arm around the young fairy. "Why don't you start at the beginning and tell me what happened?" she asked gently. She guided Cara over to a rock and sat her down.

Cara still hadn't stopped crying. "Please stop," Cocoa begged her. "If we are going to fix this mess, we have to know what happened."

Cara sniffled and took quick breaths to try to calm down. "Please don't tell Melli or Princess Lolli," she said. She looked up at Cocoa. "I really am so sorry for this mess that I've made."

"Cara, just tell me what happened," Cocoa begged. She gave Cara's shoulder a tight squeeze. "I promise I won't be mad."

Cara's shoulders relaxed and she was able to breathe easier. "Well," Cara began, "I saw your wand on the ground after Sun Dip. It was sticking out of one of the licorice bushes by Red Licorice Lake." She wiped her eyes with her hand. "I was going to give it back to you. That's why I picked it up." Her brown eyes glanced at the wand now in Cocoa's hands. "But the wand is just so beautiful."

"It's the power of chocolate," Cocoa said. "It's very hard to resist."

Cara nodded. "Yes," she agreed.

"And so you tried it out?" Cocoa asked.

"I didn't realize the magic was so strong," Cara went on. "As soon as I picked up the wand, things started to change into chocolate." The Caramel Fairy sniffled. "And the more I tried to stop that from happening, the more chocolate I made!"

Standing up, Cara walked over to the chocolate oak and leaned against the tree. "I wanted to fix what I had done, but I couldn't," she explained. "I went to find one of Raina's books. I thought I could find the answer without anyone knowing what I had done."

"Why didn't you just come to me or to Melli?" Cocoa asked.

Cara looked down at her golden brown shoes. "I wanted to fix my mess by myself," she said.

"Oh, Cara." Cocoa sighed. "You should never

be scared to tell a friend that you need help."

Pulling her hair away from her face, Cara let out a long sigh. "I guess," she said. "But at the time, I thought Raina's books could offer a quick fix." She let her hair fall around her shoulders.

"Those books don't always have the answer," Cocoa said sadly.

Cara paced around the tree. "When I got to Gummy Forest, Mogu was there!" she said. "I had never seen a troll up close before. He was so salty! I panicked and caused a chocolate explosion."

Cocoa flew over to Cara and took her hand. "Yes, I've seen Gummy Forest." She guided the young fairy back to the rock. "And then why did you go to Sour Orchard?"

"I remember hearing that Berry went to see Lemona the Sour Orchard Fairy," Cara said.

"Lemona was able to help Berry with those sour heart candies that she found by Chocolate River."

Cocoa remembered how difficult that journey had been for Berry. Berry was afraid to go to a different part of Sugar Valley. Raina had gone with her, and together they had found the Sour Orchard Fairy. And Cara, who was much younger, had gone by herself! Poor Cara, she really was trying to do everything alone.

"I didn't get very far into Sour Orchard when the wand starting oozing chocolate syrup," Cara told Cocoa. "Then I knew that I was really in a mess." She hung her head. "I heard the sugar flies buzzing about the Sugar Ball being canceled, and I got scared. I couldn't believe I had caused so much trouble. I came back here and thought I'd be safe in Chocolate Woods."

The wand in Cocoa's hands sparkled in the sunlight. The candy jewels were catching the sun's rays, and the fairy etched in the round globe was smiling. When she'd had the idea for the Sugar Ball accessory, Cocoa had never dreamed that the wand would create so many problems. Cocoa looked back at Cara's sad face.

"I thought it would be fun to try to be a Chocolate Fairy," Cara said softly. She was staring down at her hands. "At least for a little while."

"Just because you are a Caramel Fairy doesn't mean that you can't work with chocolate," Cocoa told her. "Melli and I work together all the time. But trying to make chocolate? You're going to have to leave that to the Chocolate Fairies."

Cara nodded.

"You know, when I was younger, I really wanted to be a Gummy Fairy," Cocoa told her. "I was so jealous of all the colors that Raina got to play with. Her candies were all the colors of the rainbow. Chocolate only has a few shades, you know."

"Really? You wanted to be a different kind of fairy?" Cara asked. Her eyes were wide with disbelief.

"Yes, even though I am one hundred percent chocolate!" Cocoa exclaimed. "As you can imagine, my trials didn't work out so well." She laughed to herself as she recalled her attempts. "My candies were not very good or tasty. I learned an important lesson. Candy Fairies can enjoy all kinds of candy in Sugar Valley, but when it comes to making candy, we need to stick with what comes naturally."

Cara giggled. "Well, I believe that. I can't seem to aim right or make anything except chocolate puddles!"

Cocoa was happy to see a smile appear on Cara's face. She held out her hand to her. "Come on," Cocoa said. "Let's let everyone know the wand has been found and get Sugar Valley cleaned up."

For the first time since the wand had disappeared, Cocoa had hope that the Sugar Ball still had a chance of happening.

9

Chocolate Cleanup

Cocoa stood by the chocolate oak tree and watched Cara and Melli. She wanted to give the sisters a few minutes together. After Cara had calmed down, Cocoa pleaded with her to let Melli know what had happened. Just as Cocoa expected, Melli was in Chocolate Woods in a flash once she got the sugar fly message.

Knowing Melli, she would feel terrible that Cara hadn't come to her for help.

Melli's arm was around her sister as the little fairy told her story. After they hugged, Cocoa flew over to them.

"I sent a sugar fly to Candy Castle," she told the sisters. "I wanted to let Princess Lolli know that there was no chocolate spell, just a chocolate mess." She looked at Cara. "I didn't get into all

the details," she said. "So if you want to tell her what happened, that can be your choice."

Cara smiled. "Thank you, Cocoa," she whispered. "And I promise I will tell her. I don't want her to think that any of this was your fault."

"Licking lollipops!" Berry shouted as she sprang down beside them. "I just heard the sweet news from the sugar flies. No chocolate spell!" She swooped up in the air and then landed on her feet. "But we need a cleanup crew. Sugar Valley is still chocolate-coated."

"And we're just the fairies for the cleanup job," Dash said as she landed next to Berry.

"We came as soon as we heard the good news," Raina added. She hovered above her friends.

Cocoa laughed. "You see, Cara," she said, "you always need your friends around to lend a helping hand."

"Sugar flies really do get the news out in Sugar Valley," Cara said.

"Sure as sugar!" the fairies said together, laughing.

Feeling a boost of energy, Cocoa took charge. "We should each take a part of Sugar Valley to cleanup. The faster we get the chocolate off the ground, the better the chance for the crops."

"And for making sure that the Sugar Ball happens tonight," Melli added.

The fairies all stood together in agreement.

"I'll take Gummy Forest," Raina said.

"Consider Fruit Chew Meadow cleaned," Berry said.

"Peppermint Grove will be chocolate free after I'm done!" Dash exclaimed.

"Cara and I can help out in Sour Orchard," Melli offered. She grabbed her sister's hand and gave it a tight squeeze.

"And I'll take care of Red Licorice Lake," Cocoa added.

"Sounds like we've got a plan," Melli said.

"Hopefully we'll have a Sugar Ball to attend too!" Dash said with a grin. "Now that there is no spell, we can have a party tonight."

"But first we need to make sure all the crops are safe," Cocoa said. "The chocolate puddles haven't been sitting too long, so maybe there won't be any damage."

Raina agreed. "I think we have a good chance," she said. "From what I have read, the chocolate hasn't been on the ground long enough to change the crops."

"Let's all meet back at Candy Castle at Sun Dip," Cocoa told her friends. "That should give us enough time to clean up and then talk to Princess Lolli."

"Oh, I hope she'll let us have the ball," Dash mumbled.

"Me too," Cocoa whispered.

The large orange sun touched the top of the Frosted Mountains. Cocoa was exhausted. Cleaning up after a chocolate mess was not an easy task. Every part of her body ached from the tip of her wings to the bottom of her toes. She looked around at the sugar sand shoreline of Red Licorice Lake. Not a drop of chocolate in sight. Cocoa sighed. She hoped her friends had had the same luck in their spots.

When Cocoa found her friends, they all looked just as worn out as she felt.

"Chocolate cleanup completed," Raina announced when she saw Cocoa. "There was no damage to the gummy crops that I saw."

"Fruit Chew Meadow was fine too," Berry said.

"I think everything is going to be okay," Dash agreed.

Cara stood up. "Melli and I took care of Sour Orchard," she told Cocoa. "Everything looks back to normal."

Cocoa clapped her hands. *"Choc-o-rific!"* she exclaimed.

"I'm going to talk to Princess Lolli," Cara said.

Cocoa and her friends surrounded Cara.

Princess Lolli was fair and true, but telling her something like this would be scary for the young fairy.

"We'll go with you," Cocoa told her. She knew she was speaking for all her friends.

The fairies found Princess Lolli in the royal throne room. She listened to Cara's story about finding Cocoa's wand and how she couldn't stop the chocolate from spreading all over Sugar Valley.

"I am in favor of the fairies experimenting with new candies and techniques," Princess Lolli said, "but you should always ask permission. Especially if magic is involved."

Cara nodded her head. "I promise never to try that trick again," she vowed. "From now on, I'm sticking with caramel."

"A fine choice for you," Princess Lolli told her. "You are a good Caramel Fairy, Cara. You are full of sweetness, and I know you didn't mean any harm to the kingdom."

Melli took Cara's hand. "Please don't ever feel that you can't come to me for help."

"All of us are here for you," Cocoa said. "Sure as sugar."

Cara smiled as she looked at the fairies around her. "Thank you," she said. "I promise."

Princess Lolli glanced up at the large candy clock on the wall. "Sun Dip is over, and now it's getting late." She turned to look at the other fairies. "What do you think about getting on with the Sugar Ball?"

The fairies all cheered.

"Those are some extra-sweet words!" Cocoa

cried. "I can't wait to wear my new dress." She put her hands on her hips. "But maybe I should leave my chocolate wand at home."

Everyone laughed, but Princess Lolli shook her head.

"You've worked very hard on that wand, Cocoa," the fairy princess said. "Please don't leave the wand at home."

Cocoa's wings fluttered, and she couldn't help but smile. "I would love to bring my chocolate wand tonight. And I won't be letting it out of my sight the whole night!"

10

Chocolate Dip

The grand ballroom at Candy Castle was glorious. The entire room was glowing with tiny sparkling white sugar lights. Each table was covered with a white tablecloth with tall sugar blossom branches in brightly colored gummy vases. The tiny white flowers on the branches were shimmering with colored sugar.

The room had never looked so sweet.

Cocoa twirled around in a circle in front of her friends.

"The dress is delicious," Berry remarked.

Blushing, Cocoa smoothed out the skirt. "Thank you," she said. "A comment like that from you is extra-sweet."

Across the room Cocoa saw Cara. She was wearing a short dark caramel dress with a sparkling tiara in her hair. Cocoa flew over to her and noticed that the sweet tiara was covered in tiny caramel drops.

"Your tiara is extraordinary," Cocoa told her.

Cara curtsied. "Thank you. I may not be able to handle chocolate, but I am learning how to make caramel candy!"

"Well done," Cocoa cheered.

Princess Lolli came over to Cocoa and Cara. Her pink-and-white-sugar layered dress looked scrumptious. In her left hand, Cocoa noticed the royal wand. Princess Lolli's wand was made entirely of sugar crystals. The wand was dazzling with the sugar-frosted jewels. Cocoa couldn't take her eyes off it.

"I see you did bring your chocolate wand," Princess Lolli said to Cocoa. "I'm glad that you did. Your work is excellent. You should be proud."

"Thank you," Cocoa said. "And I'm not letting the wand go!" She laughed. "No more crazy chocolate episodes in Sugar Valley."

"Let's hope not," Princess Lolli said, grinning.

Cara held her hand up to her chest. "Certainly not from me," she vowed.

Princess Lolli winked at her. "Enjoy the party,"

she said as she flew to greet more guests.

"Look," Melli cried as she raced over to Cara and Cocoa. "It's the Sugar Pops! They really are here!" She pointed to the far corner of the room, where a stage was set up.

"Where are the Sugar Pops?" Dash and Berry exclaimed from behind Melli. She looked all around.

Raina landed next to Dash. "The Sugar Pops are here already?" she asked.

Melli laughed. "They are right there," she said. She put her hands on their shoulders and faced them in the right direction.

Once everyone saw the brothers, they let out a sigh.

"Now the party can really begin," Coca said, smiling.

"Char is just so yummy," Melli said with a sigh. "Look at that hat. He is just the sweetest."

Dash flew up above her friends to get a better view. "I don't know," she said. "I think Chip is just delish."

Cocoa laughed. "Well, together those three have the best sound in Sugar Valley. Let's go say hi to them."

Melli pulled at Cocoa's hand. "Do you think they will remember us?" she asked.

"Hot chocolate!" Cocoa exclaimed. "Of course they will remember! How could they forget the fairies who saved Caramel Moon?"

The four friends laughed and followed Cocoa over to the front of the stage.

Just as Char, Carob, and Chip took center stage, Cocoa caught Char's eye. He grinned down at her and then whispered in his brothers' ears.

A hush fell over the crowd. Everyone wondered what the Sugar Pops were up to. Char grabbed the microphone and greeted the crowd.

"Hello, Candy Kingdom!" he sang out. "Happy Sugar Ball! We're so happy to be here today now that the chocolate mess has ended." A roar of cheers and applause echoed in the room. "And we'd like to call up five of our fairy friends to help us with our first song, 'Chocolate Dip.'"

"'Chocolate Dip' is my favorite song!" Cocoa exclaimed. She grabbed her friends, and they all flew to the stage. They were so excited to be close to the famous singers again. Cocoa reached out and took Cara's hand. "Come with us!" she shouted.

Char nodded and the music started. The

friends huddled together and swayed to the music. Looking out at the crowd, Cocoa saw that everyone was having a great time. She waved her wand at the end of the song, and tiny chocolates fell around the Sugar Pops. The boys laughed and threw the candies out in the crowd.

"Nice touch, Cocoa," Char whispered. "That is some wand!"

Cocoa thought her heart would melt!

"Oh, you have no idea," Melli mumbled. Laughing, Melli gave Cocoa a tight hug.

The Sugar Pops went on to play all their hits. All the fairies in the kingdom were rocking out to their sweet sounds. The Sugar Ball was a great success, and everyone was having a supersweet time.

Cocoa went over to Cara and put a chocolate

drop in her hand. "If you ever need any chocolate, please never hesitate to ask me," she said.

"Don't worry," Cara told her. "I know where to find my chocolate. You have my word that I will be more responsible."

"Sure as sugar," Cocoa said. "This is the best Sugar Ball ever!"

She twirled Cara out on the dance floor. "Maybe we can work on some caramel and chocolate candies together."

"I would love that," Cara said, smiling.

"Me too," Melli said, coming between them. "Count me in."

"Count us all in!" Dash exclaimed.

"The more fairy friends, the sweeter!" Cocoa announced. And then she fluttered her wings and spun around to the music.

A Valentine's Surprise

Raina the Gummy Fairy sprinkled handfuls of colorful flavor flakes into Gummy Lake. She smiled as the gummy fish swam over and gobbled up the food. Watching the fish eat made Raina's tummy rumble. She had gotten up very early and had been working in Gummy Forest all morning. When she settled on a perch high up on a gummy tree, Raina opened her backpack. All the animals in the forest were fed, and now she could relax and eat her own lunch.

Raina had an important job in Sugar Valley. She took care of the gummy animals that lived in Gummy Forest. There were many types of gummy animals, from friendly bear cubs to playful bunnies. Raina was fair and kind to each of the animals—and they all loved her.

"Hi, Raina!" a voice called out.

Raina looked up to see Dash, a Mint Fairy, flying in circles above her head. The small, sweet fairy glided down to see her.

"I was hoping to find you here," Dash said. "I need your help."

Raina was always willing to help out any of her friends. She had a heart that was pure sugar. "What's going on?" she asked.

Dash landed on the branch next to Raina. She peered over at the bowl in Raina's hand. Dash was small, but she always had a huge appetite!

"Hmmm, that smells good," she said. "What is that?"

"It's fruit nectar. Berry brought me some yesterday," Raina told her. She watched Dash's eyes grow wider. It wasn't hard to tell that Dash would love a taste. "Do you want to try some?" she asked.

"Thanks," Dash said, licking her lips. "Berry's nectars are always supersweet." Dash leaned over for her taste. Berry the Fruit Fairy had a flair for the fabulous. And she could whip up a spectacular nectar. "Yum," Dash continued. "Berry makes the best fruit nectar soup."

Raina laughed. "I don't think I've ever heard you say that you didn't like something a Candy Fairy made," she told her minty friend.

"Very funny," Dash said, knowing that her friend was speaking the truth.

"Have you come up with any ideas about what to get Berry?" Raina asked.

Dash flapped her wings. "That is why I'm coming to see you," she said. "I was hoping you could give me an idea. I know Berry would love something from Meringue Island, but that is a little too far. She's the only one I haven't gotten a gift for, and Valentine's Day is tomorrow. Since it's also her birthday, I want to make sure the gift is supersweet."

"Sure as sugar, Berry would love anything from Meringue Island," Raina agreed. Meringue

Island was in the Vanilla Sea and was *the* place for fashion. Berry loved fashion—especially jewelry and fancy clothes. When Fruli, a Fruit Fairy, had come to Sugar Valley from the island, Berry was very jealous of her. Fruli had beautiful clothes and knew how to put together high-fashion looks.

"The truth is," Raina added, leaning in closer to Dash. "Berry would like anything you gave her."

"But I want to give her something she is really going to love," Dash replied. She swung her legs back and forth. "I want to surprise her with a special gift this year." Her silver wings flapped quickly. "I wish I could think of something with extra sugar!"

"I know how you feel," Raina said. "I've had the hardest time coming up with an idea." She looked over at Dash. "I'll tell you what I'm going to get her, but please keep it a secret."

"Sure as sugar!" Dash exclaimed. She clapped her hands. "Oh, what are you planning?"

Raina took her last sip of the fruit nectar. "Last night I was reading a story in the Fairy Code Book, and I got a delicious idea."

Dash rolled her eyes. "I should have guessed that this would have something to do with the Fairy Code Book," she said.

Raina read the Fairy Code Book so often that her friends teased her that she knew the whole book by heart.

"Well," Raina continued, "there is a great story in the book about Lyra, the Fruit Chew Meadow unicorn."

"Oh, I love Lyra," Dash sang out. "She grows

those gorgeous candy flowers at the edge of the meadow." Just as she said those words, Dash knew why Raina's grin was so wide. "You talked to Lyra, and she is going to give you a special flower for Berry?"

Raina laughed. "Dash!" she said. "You ruined my surprise." She put her empty bowl back inside her bag. "I thought that if I got Berry a flower, I could make a headband for her. You know how she loves to accessorize."

"The more the better, for Berry," Dash added. "And those are the fanciest flowers in the kingdom. *So mint!* Berry is going to love that headband." Dash stopped talking for a moment to take in the whole idea. "Wait, how'd you get Lyra to do that for you? Unicorns don't like to talk to anyone!"

Raina smiled. "Well, that's not really true," she said.

"Let me guess," Dash said. "Did you read that in a book?"

Raina giggled. "Actually, I didn't," she told her friend. "To be honest, I think Lyra is just shy."

"Really?" Dash asked. "Can I meet her? Maybe she'll have another idea for a gift for Berry. Let's go now." She stood up and leaped off the branch into the air.

"I've been working all morning," Raina said. She reached her arms up into a wide stretch. "Maybe we can go in a little while?"

Dash fluttered back down to the branch. Her small silver wings flapped quickly. "Come on," she begged. "Let's go now!"

Dash was known for being fast on the

slopes of the Frosted Mountains—and for being impatient. She liked to move quickly and make fast decisions.

Leaning back on the gummy tree, Raina closed her eyes. "Please just let me rest a little, and then we can go," she said with a yawn.

"All right," Dash said. "Do you have any more of that nectar?"

Raina gave Dash her bowl and poured out some more of Berry's nectar. Then she shut her eyes. Before Raina drifted off to sleep, she imagined Berry's happy face when she saw her birthday present. Sure as sugar, Valentine's Day was going to be supersweet!

Candy Fairies

Read all the books
in the Candy Fairies series!

Visit
candyfairies.com
for more delicious
fun with your
favorite fairies.

Play games, download activities,
and so much more!

From Aladdin

PUBLISHED BY SIMON & SCHUSTER

Nancy Drew and the Clue Crew

Test your detective skills with more Clue Crew cases!

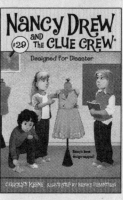

From Aladdin • Published by Simon & Schuster

The Faeries' Promise

Read all the books in the series!

Read The Unicorn's Secret, the series that started it all.

From Aladdin · Published by Simon & Schuster

Magic Hearts

READ ALL THE CANDY FAIRIES BOOKS!

Chocolate Dreams

Rainbow Swirl

Caramel Moon

Cool Mint

COMING SOON:

Gooey Goblins

The Sugar Ball

Candy Fairies

Magic Hearts

HELEN PERELMAN

ILLUSTRATED BY
ERICA-JANE WATERS

ALADDIN
NEW YORK   LONDON   TORONTO   SYDNEY

This book is a work of fiction. Any references to historical events, real people, or
real locales are used fictitiously. Other names, characters, places, and incidents are the
product of the author's imagination, and any resemblance to actual events or locales or
persons, living or dead, is entirely coincidental.

ALADDIN

An imprint of Simon & Schuster Children's Publishing Division

1230 Avenue of the Americas, New York, NY 10020

First Aladdin paperback edition January 2011

Text copyright © 2011 by Helen Perelman Bernstein

Illustrations copyright © 2011 by Erica-Jane Waters

All rights reserved, including the right of reproduction in whole or in part in any form.

ALADDIN is a trademark of Simon & Schuster, Inc., and related logo is a registered
trademark of Simon & Schuster, Inc.

For information about special discounts for bulk purchases, please contact
Simon & Schuster Special Sales at 1-866-506-1949 or business@simonandschuster.com.

The Simon & Schuster Speakers Bureau can bring authors to your live event.

For more information or to book an event contact the Simon & Schuster

Speakers Bureau at 1-866-248-3049 or visit our website at www.simonspeakers.com.

Designed by Karin Paprocki

The text of this book was set in Berthold Baskerville Book.

Manufactured in the United States of America

1113 OFF

4 6 8 10 9 7 5

Library of Congress Control Number 2010002494

ISBN 978-1-4424-0823-4

ISBN 978-1-4424-0824-1 (eBook)

For Danielle, my sweet niece!

Contents

Magic Hearts

CHAPTER 1

A New Fairy Friend

What do you think?" Berry held up a string
of colorful fruit chews. The Fruit Fairy enjoyed
making delicious fruit candies, but she also loved
making jewelry. The more sparkle the better!
Berry loved anything and everything to do with
fashion.

"Berry," Raina said. She had a worried look

 1

on her face. The Gummy Fairy was filling up a bottle of cherry syrup for the trees in Gummy Forest. She had come to Fruit Chew Meadow for flavoring for the red gumdrop trees—and to visit Berry. But instead of finding Berry working on her fruit candies, her friend was making a necklace!

"Those are round chews," Raina said. "Where are the hearts?"

Berry shrugged. "These round fruit chews are just so pretty," she said with a heavy sigh. She held up the colorful strand again and admired the rainbow pattern she had made. "I just had to make a necklace with them!" She carefully knotted the end of the string. Then she put on a special caramel clasp that Melli, her Caramel Fairy friend, had made for her. Berry placed the finished necklace around her neck. She proudly spread her pink wings as she showed off her newest creation.

"Berry, Heart Day is coming up," Raina said gently. After she put the cap on the syrup bottle, she looked up at her friend. "Everyone in Sugar Valley is busy making candy hearts. And you're stringing round chews! You don't want to disappoint Princess Lolli, do you?"

Berry dragged her foot along the ground. There was a layer of powdered sugar that had fallen during the evening. It was a cold winter's day in Sugar Valley. The cool winds were blowing, and there was a chill in the air. "Sweet strawberries!" Berry exclaimed. "I would never want to upset Princess Lolli!"

Princess Lolli was the ruling fairy princess of Candy Kingdom. She was a caring and gentle fairy, and always treated the fairies very well. All the fairies loved her and wanted to please her. The sweet princess's favorite shape was a heart, so every fairy in the kingdom made special candy hearts from flavors found all over Sugar Valley. There were chocolate, gummy, mint, caramel, and fruit heart candies for Princess Lolli and the fairies to enjoy. Heart Day was a happy day, filled with good cheer—and delicious candy.

"I still have time to make something for Princess Lolli," Berry said. "Last year she loved my red fruit hearts, remember? I put a fruit surprise in each one and sprinkled them with red sugar."

Raina nodded. "Yes, and you spent weeks making those. Don't forget that Heart Day is next week."

"I will start on something today," Berry declared.

At that moment another Fruit Fairy flew up to the friends. Berry had just met her the other day. Her name was Fruli, and she was new to Sugar Valley. She had long blond hair, and today she was wearing the most beautiful dress

Berry had ever seen. There were tiny purple and pink candies sewn along the collar and cuffs that sparkled in the sun. Over her dress was a soft cape made of pink-and-white cotton candy. The fairy soared down next to them with her pale pink wings.

"Hi," Raina said. "You must be new here."

"This is Fruli," Berry said, introducing Raina to the newest Fruit Fairy. "She's from Meringue Island."

"Welcome to Sugar Valley," Raina said. "I've never been to Meringue Island, but I've read about the place. There's a story in the Fairy Code Book about the majestic Meringue Mountains. I've heard the island is beautiful and is the center of fashion." She smiled at Berry. "Berry loves fashion too."

Berry blushed. "Raina loves to read," she quickly explained. "She's memorized the Fairy Code Book."

Raina laughed. "Well, I do like to read. What about you, Fruli?"

"Yes, I like to read," she said very softly. She looked down at her white boots. Her response was so quiet that Berry and Raina could barely hear her.

"I love your cape," Raina said tentatively, eyeing the fabric and design. "Is that from Meringue Island?"

Fruli nodded. "Yes," she said. She didn't raise her eyes from the ground. "I'm sorry to interrupt."

Again, her voice was so low and soft, Berry and Raina could barely hear her.

"I just came to collect a couple of fruit chews for Princess Lolli," Fruli said.

"Well, you came to the right place," Raina said, smiling. She gave Berry a little push forward. She wondered why her friend was being so quiet around this new fairy. Usually, Berry was very outgoing and not shy at all. "Berry grows the best fruit chews on this side of the Frosted Mountains." She put her arm around her friend.

"Raina," Berry mumbled, feeling embarrassed. She smoothed her dress with her hands and noticed a big cherry syrup stain on the front.

Oh no, Berry thought. *What a big mess! Fruli has the nicest clothes. And look at me!*

"These chews?" Fruli asked, pointing.

"Yes," Berry said. "Please take anything you want."

Fruli took a few candies and put them in a white chocolate weave bag. "Thank you," she said.

Before Berry or Raina could say a word, she flew off.

"She was so shy!" Raina exclaimed.

"Did you see her clothes?" Berry asked. "She has the nicest outfits. I have *got* to get moving on making a new dress for Heart Day."

"Berry—," Raina started to say.

"I know," Berry said, holding up her hand. "I will make the heart candies, but I also need to find something new to wear to Candy Castle for Heart Day."

Berry flew off in a hurry, leaving Raina standing in Fruit Chew Meadow alone. Raina was worried. When Berry got an idea stuck in her head, sometimes things got a little sticky.

2

Wild Cherry

Berry sat in front of two large pieces of fruit-dyed fabric. Bright pinks and reds were swirled around the material in large circles. Berry had been saving the material for something special, and a new outfit for Heart Day was the perfect occasion!

For a week she had tried drawing designs

for a new dress. Normally, designing a dress was fun and exciting for her. But this time nothing seemed right. To make things a little more sour, none of her friends understood her passion for fashion. Raina kept asking about heart candies, and her other friends did not seem interested in her dress designs. Berry sighed as she picked up the chalk to sketch out the dress form.

"I wish I could go to Meringue Island," she mumbled to herself. Even though the material in her hand was silky smooth, she was still feeling unsure. If only she could fly to the small, exclusive Meringue Island, she could buy a bunch of stylish new outfits. Meringue Island was known for high fashion and tons of cool accessories. Fruli probably thought all the fairies in Sugar Valley dressed terribly. Berry looked down at her red shiny dress. She used to love this one, but after seeing Fruli's dresses, she felt sloppy and very plain.

Berry didn't want to think about the beautiful dress that Fruli would be wearing on Heart Day. Thinking of what Fruli would wear made her face scrunch up like she had eaten a sour lemon ball.

I'll show her that Sugar Valley fairies know fashion and accessories too! Berry thought. She smoothed out the fabric and took out her scissors.

Her new dress was going to be the nicest one she'd ever made!

With thin caramel thread, Berry skillfully sewed up the dress. For extra sparkle, she added some of her new fruit chews around the collar.

She stood back and admired the dress. A smile spread across her face.

"Straight from the runways of Meringue Island," she said, pretending to be an announcer. "We are proud to carry the designs of Berry the Fruit Fairy!"

Berry slipped into the dress and spun around. Giggling, she felt so happy and glamorous. All her hard work had paid off.

Looking up at the sky, Berry noted the sun getting closer to the Frosted Mountains. Once the sun hit the top, Sun Dip would begin. At the end of the day her fairy friends gathered on the shores of Red Licorice Lake. They shared stories and snacked on candy. Usually, Berry was the last fairy to arrive.

Maybe today I'll surprise them, she thought. *I can be the first one there!*

She checked herself in the mirror and then flew out over the valley to Red Licorice Lake.

As she flew, Berry wished she had candy hearts for Princess Lolli. If the candies were finished, she'd have more time to make accessories for her new outfit. Berry smiled to herself. After all, accessories were the key to fashion! Maybe she could add a shawl, or even a cape? She had read all the fashion magazines and flipped through this season's catalogs. She could come up with something fabulous!

Seeing the tall spirals of Candy Castle off in the distance made Berry's heart sink. She realized she couldn't go to Heart Day empty-handed! She desperately needed a heart-shaped candy for the fairy princess.

Just then something red caught her eye. Down by the shores of Chocolate River there was something red and shiny glistening in the sun. Curious, Berry flew down to check out what was there. As she got closer, she saw that there was a small vine growing in the brown sugar sand.

"How odd," Berry said. Usually, there were some chocolate flowers growing there, but this vine looked different. She peered down closely at the plant. Berry couldn't believe her eyes! On the vine were tiny red hearts!

"Licking lollipops!" she cried out.

She reached down and plucked one of the hearts off the tiny vine.

Berry couldn't believe her luck. She was just wishing for candy hearts, and then they appeared!

These must be magic hearts, she thought.

Holding the heart in her hand, Berry examined the tiny candy. The rosy red color made her believe that these were cherry flavored. A bonus that cherry was one of Princess Lolli's favorite flavors. Carefully, Berry picked the hearts off the vine and placed them in her basket. Now she had something for Heart Day—and had time to finish her outfit!

After her basket was full, Berry flew over to Red Licorice Lake. It was the perfect day for her to be early for Sun Dip. She had lots to share with her friends today. She had news of her latest dress design, and magic heart candies for Princess Lolli. Maybe today wasn't so sour after all! Sweet wild cherry magic hearts just saved the day.

CHAPTER 3

Sweet Hearts

Berry spread her blanket on the red sugar sand and waited for her friends to arrive. The sun was just hitting the white tips of the mountains, and she knew that soon her friends would be there.

Dash the Mint Fairy was the first to arrive. Dash was the smallest Mint Fairy in the kingdom, but she had the biggest appetite!

"Berry, what are you doing here so early?" Dash cried as she swept down to the ground. She eyed Berry's new outfit. "You look fantastic. Is that a new dress?"

Smiling, Berry nodded. "I just made it!" she exclaimed.

"So mint!" Dash said. "I love the colors."

Cocoa the Chocolate Fairy and Melli the Caramel Fairy flew up next.

"Is this a special Sun Dip?" Melli asked. She looked Berry up and down. "You are wearing such a fancy dress."

"Hot chocolate! Where did you get that?" Cocoa asked, amazed. "It's fabulous."

Berry was enjoying all her friends' reactions to her new outfit. She stood up and spun in a circle. "It is pretty, don't you think?"

"I do," Melli said. "But I didn't get a sugar fly message about dressing up for tonight."

Berry laughed. "I just wanted to show you all my new outfit for Heart Day," she said.

"Yum!" Dash cheered. "I can't wait for Heart Day. I made the most delicious mint hearts, and Cocoa has promised to dip them in dark chocolate for me."

"That's right," Cocoa added. "Mint and chocolate hearts are an excellent combination." The two friends high-fived.

Dash turned to Melli. She knew that Melli and Cocoa often worked together, but this year Melli wanted to work on her own heart candies. "What did you make?"

A smile appeared on Melli's face. She dipped

her hand in her basket and pulled out a delicate heart.

"Is that caramel?" Dash asked, coming closer. She looked at the fragile heart in Melli's hand. The dark caramel looked like fine thread, but the candy was hard and didn't break when she touched it.

"That looks like imported lace!" Berry said. She leaned in to get a better look. "Melli, that is beautiful work."

"How long did that take you to make?" Dash asked.

Cocoa put her arm around Melli. "I told you these hearts were truly special," she told her.

Melli grinned. "Thank you," she said. "I've been working on these candies for weeks. I just hope Princess Lolli likes them."

"She's going to love those hearts," Dash told her. Then she licked her lips. "Maybe I should just try one to make sure they taste okay?"

"Dash!" Melli scolded. But then she started to laugh. "I knew you'd say that, so I brought some extra for tonight."

Dash's face brightened. "Ah, you are a good friend, Melli," she replied. Then she took a bite of the caramel heart. "Sweetheart, that is a *sweet heart*!" she said, laughing.

"Thank you," Melli said, and blushed.

"Wow, Berry!" Raina cried as she swooped down to her friends. "You have been working hard." She settled herself down on the blanket that Berry had spread out for the fairies. "The dress is beautiful. A true original."

Berry was bursting with pride.

"If you had time to make that dress, you must have finished your candy, right?" Raina asked.

Berry looked over at Raina. She had expected that Raina would say something like that. And she was ready! "Actually, I do have my heart candy," she replied. She placed her basket of tiny red hearts in the center of her blanket. Though she had not worked as hard on her candy as Melli, Berry was still excited to show off the new candy.

The fairies all moved closer to the basket.

"*So mint*!" Dash shouted. "Berry, you *do* have hearts for Princess Lolli!" She turned to look at Raina. "And you were worried about Berry. See, I told you she'd come through."

Berry hugged Dash. "Thanks, Dash," she said.

"You managed to make a dress and these

candies?" Melli asked. She peered into the basket. "That's very impressive, Berry."

Cocoa shook her head. "It takes me weeks to get chocolate hearts right," she said. "Hearts are the hardest shapes to make!"

"Well," Berry said. She was about to confess that she had found the candy, but then she held back.

Raina fluttered her wings. She peered down at the red candies. "There's something very familiar about these hearts," she said. She took the Fairy Code Book out of her bag. She placed the thick volume on the ground and quickly flipped through the pages. "I know I've seen those candies before." She didn't look up at her friends. She continued to thumb through the pages.

Dash reached over to the basket. "What flavor are they, Berry?"

"Cherry, of course," Berry stated proudly. "Princess Lolli's favorite flavor!"

Dash popped a heart in her mouth. Her blue eyes grew wide, and her wings flapped so fast she shot straight up in the air. "Holy peppermint!" she cried.

"What's wrong?" Cocoa exclaimed, reaching up to grab Dash. "Are you all right?"

"Those are not sweet hearts!" she said, scrunching up her face. "Those are sour wild cherry hearts!"

All the fairies gasped. Berry's hands flew to her mouth. Her not-so-sweet hearts had suddenly made Sun Dip very sour.

4

Sour Surprise

Berry shuddered. She felt awful about lying to her friends. She didn't know much about sour candy. She only knew that some was grown in Sour Orchard. While many fairies enjoyed the sweet-and-sour crops from the orchard at the far end of Sugar Valley, Berry did not. She preferred the sweet, fruity flavors of her own candy.

"Are you okay?" Berry asked Dash. She went over to her and put her hand on her friend's back. Dash's silver wings fluttered and brushed Berry's hand.

"Yes," Dash said. "I'm fine. I like those sour candies." She licked her fingers.

"Leave it to Dash to like just about any candy!" Cocoa said, giggling. "Even the most sour."

Dash shrugged her shoulders and looked over at Berry. "I just wasn't expecting that from a candy *you* grew," she said. "Those hearts looked so sweet and delicious."

Berry hung her head. "Well, I didn't grow these," she admitted, looking down at the ground. "I picked them from the bank of Chocolate River. They were beautiful—and heart-shaped."

"So you have no idea where these came from?" Melli asked. Her hand flew to her gaping mouth. "You don't know what these candies are made of?"

"And you didn't even test them first?" Cocoa added, amazed. "What happens if the hearts are poisonous or something horrible!"

"Cocoa!" Melli said. She never liked when her friends argued. She could tell that Cocoa's comment was making Berry upset. She turned her attention to Dash. "She looks the same. Are you feeling okay?"

"Stop looking at me like that!" Dash cried. "The hearts were good." She reached out toward Berry's basket.

"Dash!" all the fairies said at the same time.

Berry grabbed her basket away.

"Cool down," Dash said. She sat on the ground next to Raina.

Suddenly Raina gasped. While her friends had been talking, she had been carefully reading the Fairy Code Book. "I knew those heart candies looked familiar," she said. She pointed to a picture at the bottom of the page. "Look here," she instructed.

The fairy friends all leaned over the book. There was a picture of the heart candies. And next to the picture was a drawing of Lemona, a Sour Orchard Fairy.

"Are they dangerous?" Cocoa asked.

"Don't be so dark," Melli said. She kneeled down closer to the book.

"Maybe they are magic because they simply

appear when someone wishes for heart candies?" Berry said hopefully.

"Or maybe the hearts will make me fly faster down the mountain on my sled!" Dash exclaimed. She flew up in the air and did a high dive back down to the ground. "Wouldn't that be *so mint?*"

Berry knew that speeding down the Frosted Mountain trails was one of Dash's favorite things to do. Nothing would make her Mint Fairy friend happier than being the fastest fairy in the valley. She was already the smallest—and one of the fastest. While Dash flew in circles up in the air, Berry studied the Fairy Code Book. Her eyes grew wide as she read the rest of the information. She peered back up at Dash.

Sweet syrup! she thought. *What a sticky mess!*

Why hadn't she tested the candies? How could she have been so lazy? One of the first rules of making candy was that every fairy had to know the source of the ingredients. Berry's wings drooped lower to the ground as she read more about the magic hearts.

Dash came down and stood next to Berry's blanket. Berry wanted to tell her how sorry she was for what she had done. She had never meant to hurt Dash. She turned to her friend. But when Berry saw what was in front of her, she was speechless. Her mouth gaped open, and her eyes didn't budge from the sight in front of her.

"Why is everyone looking at me like that?" Dash asked. She saw the worried expressions on the faces in front of her.

The Fairy Code Book had used the words "might happen" to describe the effects of the candy. But something was *definitely* happening to Dash!

Dash's skin was bright yellow!

CHAPTER
5

A Big Heart

O h, Dash!" Berry cried out. She couldn't bear to see her friend a bright yellow color!

It was not often that fairies changed colors. Berry could think of one other time that had happened. A few years ago many of the fairies got the sugar flu. The virus was awful. Fairies couldn't fly or make any candy, and several fairies turned scarlet from the high fever. Princess Lolli set up stations in the castle for the sick fairies. Luckily, Berry, Melli, and Cocoa hadn't gotten the flu. But Dash and Raina had. Berry sighed. At least they were able to take medicine and get better. There were no viruses or germs to blame here.

This was all Berry's fault.

No one said anything. Dash fluttered her wings.

"Why is everyone staring at me?" she snapped.

"Well, she's certainly acting like the same old Dash," Cocoa said, watching the Mint Fairy.

"She doesn't look affected at all," Melli added. She shook her head in disbelief. "Except for the fact that she is now yellow."

"Yellow?" Dash screeched. "I'm yellow? As in

lemon frosting and lemon drops?" She looked down at her body and screamed.

Berry reached into her bag and gave Dash a small compact mirror. "Lemon yellow," Berry said sadly. "Take a look in the mirror. You'll see the color is all over your face."

Dash opened the candy-jeweled case and peered into the mirror. "A yellow Mint Fairy?" she cried. She snapped the mirror shut. Panicked, Dash grabbed Raina's hand. "Please tell me this will go away." When there was no reply from Raina, Dash took a deep breath. "Well, is there any medicine I can take? There must be something to make this go away, right?" She examined her yellow arms and hands.

Raina flipped through some more pages of the Fairy Code Book. "I can't find anything

more here in the book," she said. "It's odd. The book only mentions a slight change of coloring. I wonder why the bright yellow?"

"If Raina doesn't know the answer, this must be bad," Cocoa whispered to Melli.

"There is no medicine for magic spells," Melli said. "Oh, Dash . . ."

"Melli is right," Raina added. "We'll need to figure out the magic before you can get better."

"Why yellow?" Dash balked. "Blech!"

"There's only one way to fix this," Berry said. She stood up. "I have to go ask Lemona about her candy. If she's the fairy who made the candy, she'll know the answer to this riddle."

"What?" Dash said. "You, Berry the sweet and beautiful Fruit Fairy, want to venture into Sour Orchard?"

Dash might have been mocking Berry, but there was truth to what she was saying. Berry enjoyed fine fashions and sparkly accessories and was not one for flying out of her comfortable sweet spots.

"What if Lemona is as sour as her candy?" Melli asked.

"Oh, how awful," Cocoa said. "Do you think she could be like Mogu?"

"Mogu is a salty old troll who lives in Black Licorice Swamp," Raina said, shaking her head. "Lemona is one of us, a Candy Fairy."

"A Candy Fairy who lives in Sour Orchard," Melli mumbled.

Dash flew around in circles. "This color can't last, can it?" she asked. When no one answered, Dash landed and hung her head.

"Holy peppermint," she whispered. "I'll be the joke of Sugar Valley."

Berry took Dash's hand. "Don't get upset, Dash," she said. "I am going to find a way to help you. I promise."

"You'd really go to Sour Orchard for me?" Dash asked. She peered up at Berry.

"I should never have neglected my candy duties," Berry admitted. She folded her knees up to her chest. "If I hadn't been so concerned about making a new dress, then I would have made time to grow my own candy hearts for Heart Day." She gazed at Dash. "And I should have told the truth about those heart candies. Will you forgive me?"

"I'm not mad," Dash said. "I understand." She stuck her hand in her backpack. "Here, take these peppermint candies. It's getting dark and you might need light in Sour Orchard."

"Thank you," Berry told her. Dash might have been small, but she had the biggest heart of all. "I am truly sorry."

Suddenly Raina shot up from her spot on the blanket. "Oh, I found something more here," she said. She pointed to a section in the Fairy Code Book.

"I don't think I've ever been so grateful for that book," Dash said. She moved closer to Raina.

"When visiting Sour Orchard," Raina began to read, "you should bring a gift to a Sour Orchard Fairy. Sour Orchard Fairies are fond of fresh fruit blossoms."

Berry smiled. "I know where to get some

fresh and delicious orange blossoms!"

Even though it was winter in Sugar Valley, the orange trees were blossoming. The magic orange trees produced tangy and sweet candy fruit all year. Fruit Fairies took the oranges and dipped the slices into chocolate or made sweet fruit nectar for candies throughout the valley. Just that morning Berry had flown by the orange trees along the edge of Fruit Chew Meadow. Their sweet citrus smell always made her smile. It seemed even Sour Orchard Fairies enjoyed the fresh scents and tastes of the blossoms.

"Going to Sour Orchard with something to make Lemona happy will make the journey easier," Berry said.

"I'll go with you," Raina told her.

"You will?" Berry asked. "I thought you were angry at me."

Raina closed her book and slipped it back into her backpack. "I can see you are very sorry," she said. "And I don't want you to go by yourself. It's always better to fly with a friend."

Feeling overwhelmed, Berry reached out to hug her friend. "You are a good friend, Raina. Thank you."

"Melli and I will stay with Dash," Cocoa said. "I have some chocolate dots here that should keep her happy for a while."

"Thanks," Dash said. "But I don't really feel like eating right now."

Hearing Dash refuse candy made Berry move a little faster. Dash never declined a piece of candy!

"We'll go now," Berry told her. "We'll be back before bedtime. I promise you won't go to sleep a yellow Mint Fairy." She gave Dash a big hug and then waved to Melli and Cocoa. She was glad they'd be with Dash to look after her.

Together, Berry and Raina flew off toward Fruit Chew Meadow to gather orange blossoms for Lemona. Berry hoped with all her heart that the meeting would go well—and that Lemona could help get Dash back to normal. Otherwise, Heart Day was not going to be a happy day.

6

Spooky Meadow

When Berry and Raina arrived at Fruit Chew Meadow, the sun had just slid to the other side of the Frosted Mountains. Berry flew over to the row of orange trees along the side of the meadow. The sweet citrus scent smelled delicious. Being in the meadow made Berry feel safe and relaxed. But she didn't have time to rest! If they wanted to talk to Lemona before the evening stars came out, she and Raina would have to hurry.

"How can anyone be mean *and* like orange blossoms?" Berry asked Raina. She put her nose close to the beautiful orange flower.

"Mmmm," Raina said. She flew over to Berry and smelled the flower candy. "I know what you mean. Sure as sugar, these do smell sweet." She thought for a moment and then looked up at Berry. "Maybe Sour Orchard Fairies aren't as sour as their candy. You know in the Fairy Code Book there is no mention of what the Sour Orchard Fairies are like—just the kind of candy they grow."

Berry raised her eyebrows. "Have you ever met a Sour Orchard Fairy?" she asked Raina.

"No," Raina said slowly. "I've only seen one once, at Candy Castle last year at Candy Fair. She had green wings and a light green dress. I think she brought sour apple suckers to the castle."

Berry nodded. She remembered the fair last year, when all the fairies in the valley came to the summer celebration in the Royal Gardens. There were a few Sour Orchard Fairies there, but Berry hadn't talked to them. "They always look so . . ." She searched for the right word.

"Sour?" Raina asked, giggling. "I guess we don't really know, if we've never spoken to them." She helped Berry pick a few more blossoms from the tree. "Maybe we'll find out that Lemona is really a sweet fairy."

Berry put a bunch of the fragrant blossoms

in her basket. "Or maybe the Fairy Code Book suggests taking the blossoms to make sure the fairies don't get sour when a visitor comes." Her wings shook as she imagined having to face a sour fairy.

"Oh, Berry, your dress!" Raina cried.

Looking down, Berry saw orange stains on her new dress. "Oh, it's just as well," she said. "This dress wasn't really working for me anyway."

"Wait, did you just hear something rustling over there?" Raina asked, pointing to the ground. She squinted in the dark. "I don't like being here after Sun Dip."

"That must have been the wind," Berry told her. She flew down to the ground and looked around the trunk of the tree. "No one's here."

"Then where is that light coming from?" Raina asked, quivering. There was an eerie green glow getting closer and closer to the orange tree.

Berry turned around. Out of the darkness a fairy appeared.

"Aaaaah!" Berry and Raina screamed.

"Sorry," Fruli answered. "I didn't mean to scare you." She pointed her glowing peppermint candy at the ground. "I didn't think anyone would be here now," she said very softly.

Raina gasped. "Oh, Fruli!" she exclaimed. "You scared the sugar out of me!" Her hand flew to her chest. Her heart was beating so fast she could hardly breathe. "What are you doing here?"

Fruli's wings began to beat even faster. "I . . . I . . . I like to come here when the day is over and smell the orange blossoms. The sweet smell

helps me to sleep. There are orange trees like this on Meringue Island, and the smell reminds me of home."

Berry was trying to get Raina's attention. She didn't want her mentioning to Fruli what they were doing. All Berry needed was for Fruli to know that she had picked sour wild cherry hearts—and given them to one of her best friends. Worse yet, she couldn't let her know that Dash was yellow because of her!

"We have to get going," Berry said quickly. She grabbed a shawl from her bag and covered her stained dress. Then she pulled on Raina's hand and took her to the other side of the meadow.

"Berry!" Raina cried. "We didn't even say good-bye. Why are you acting so rude?"

"Did you forget about Dash? She's yellow!

I'm just trying to get to Lemona as soon as possible," Berry explained.

"Fruli seems so nice," Raina said, shaking her head. "You could have at least asked her what she did for Sun Dip. Maybe she'd want to hang out with us. She seemed homesick."

"She's too fancy. She wouldn't want to hang out with us," Berry said. "Did you see her dress?" She sighed wistfully. "She has the most glamorous clothes. She'd never want to have Sun Dip with us. She'd want to be up at the castle or with the older Fruit Fairies."

Raina eyed her friend. "Maybe, but maybe not. Have you ever asked her?"

"Why are you on her side?" Berry snapped.

"I'm not," Raina said. "I just think you could have been a little sweeter to Fruli."

Berry huffed and rolled her eyes. "Raina, she's not some lost gummy cub." She packed up the orange blossoms and looked up at Raina. "What? I'm just saying that she's fine and we're late. Come on!"

Raina shook her head. When Berry had a mission, she was focused. She knew her Fruit Fairy friend could be stubborn. She was all juiced up. "Let's get going," Raina said. "I think we have enough orange blossoms for Lemona now."

Taking flight, Berry soared through the air. She had never ventured past Chocolate River to Sour Orchard. Being there at night made things seem even spookier. She hoped with all her heart that Lemona would tell them how they could help Dash. As Berry glided over the valley with

Raina, she held tightly to her basket of orange blossoms. If the sweet smell didn't sway the sour fairy, she hoped she and Raina could. She just had to have the answer that would help Dash. Berry's heart was breaking just thinking about Dash's being yellow. This plan had to work!

7

Brave Hearts

Sour Orchard was bursting with lemon, lime, cherry, apple, and orange trees. But these trees were different from the ones Berry and Raina were used to seeing in Fruit Chew Meadow and Gummy Forest. These trees grew in the tangy sugar crystals of Sour Orchard. Thick tree trunks held up heavy branches filled with sweet and sour fruits.

Berry peered down at the orchard. "I wish it wasn't so dark," she said.

"I know," Raina said. "It's a little spooky here. But at least there's some moonlight."

"Let's fly lower so we can see better," Berry called. The orchard was much larger than Berry thought it would be. Even in the dim light, she could see that there were several rows of trees.

As she flew Berry looked at all the fruits on the trees. The thought of eating those sour candies made her mouth water. There were trees dripping with bunches of sour candy suckers and fruits.

Berry knew Fruit Chew Meadow so well that even in the dark she could find her way, but this place was different. The trees looked different and the smells were not the same.

"Thanks for coming with me," Berry whispered to Raina. She grabbed her hand. "I'm sorry I snapped at you before."

"It's okay," Raina said. "Besides, I wouldn't have let you come alone."

"You are a good friend," Berry told her. She squeezed her friend's hand tighter.

Berry spotted a familiar vine growing on a tree deep in the orchard. She pulled Raina along as she swooped down to look.

"Raina!" she exclaimed. "This is the same vine that was growing by Chocolate River! This is the magic heart vine!"

Berry landed next to the vine, and Raina followed. "Sure as sugar!" she said. "I knew those candies were magic hearts." She looked around. "Lemona must live somewhere around here."

Taking a walk around a lemon tree, Berry searched for a sign of the Sour Fairy. Her red boots crunched on the sour sugar coating the ground. "What does the Fairy Code Book say? What type of home does she have?"

"Look!" Raina exclaimed. She pointed to a sign on a lemon tree a few feet away. A small piece of fruit leather had "Lemona" etched on it. "She must live over there."

Lemona's house! Berry's heart began to race. She wasn't sure what to say to the fairy, but she knew she had to talk to her. She had to confess that she had given the candy to her friend without testing it first. As hard as that would be, Berry knew she had to find out the truth about the candy. And the secret of the magic hearts.

Before they stepped closer to the tree, a small sugar fly flew up to Berry. The messenger buzzed around her ears.

"You have a message for me?" Berry asked.

The sugar fly nodded and handed her the note. Immediately, Berry saw that the note was from Melli. Her breath caught in her chest and she gasped. "Oh, Raina! What if something horrible has happened?" she cried. Berry's wings started to flutter and she flew up in the air. "I will never forgive myself if something has happened to Dash. What was I thinking, giving out candy that I didn't know about!"

Raina touched Berry's arm. "Let's see what

61

the note says. We don't know what this is about yet."

Berry's hand was shaking. "I can't," she said, handing the note to Raina. "Would you please read this for me? I can't bear to read any more sour news today."

"Maybe the news isn't bad," Raina said. She tried to smile encouragingly at her friend.

"Please read it," Berry pleaded.

Raina opened the letter. "Dash is fine," she read. "But she is now orange! Please hurry and send along any information that you get." Raina looked up from the note. "Oh, sugar," she said. "This is worse than I thought."

Berry's eyes grew wide. "What do you mean?" she gasped.

"Well, she's turning more than one color,"

Raina said. "That's not a good sign."

Berry turned to see the sugar fly. He was waiting for a return note. Quickly, Berry scribbled a message back to her friends. "We'll soon be on our way with help," she said as she wrote the note. "Hold on. We've just arrived at the orchard." She folded up the note and handed it to the sugar fly. "Please give this to Melli or Cocoa," she instructed the sugar fly.

"Are you all right?" Raina asked, looking at Berry.

Suddenly Berry was juiced up. Dash needed her help, and she was going to get her out of this sour mess. She wasn't going to be afraid. She was simply going to ask Lemona what was in her candy and how to help get Dash back to normal.

"Let's not dip our wings in syrup yet!" Berry said. She put her hands on her hips, charged with confidence. "We're here, aren't we? We need to have brave hearts!"

Raina grinned. Her spunky friend was back! And just in time. If they were going to talk to Lemona, they needed to be brave and confident.

"Lemona will help us," Berry said. With a burst of hope, she walked toward Lemona's tree.

Just then a cloud passed over the full moon, blocking the bright moonlight for a brief moment. Berry and Raina stood still in the middle of Sour Orchard, unsure of what to do. They were so close to Lemona's tree, but they couldn't see a thing!

CHAPTER

8

Sweet Sours

Licking lollipops!" Berry cried. "It's too dark!" How could they talk to Lemona if they couldn't find her front door?

"Wait," Raina said. "I have those peppermint candies that Dash gave us before we left." She dug around into her bag and pulled out a bright candy.

Berry smiled. "When we get back, we'll have to thank Dash for giving those to us," she said.

In the pale green light of the glowing peppermint, the two fairies were able to find their way to Lemona's tree.

Berry paused before knocking on the door. There was a strong scent of lemon in the air, and Berry turned to Raina. "Ready?" she asked.

"If you are," the Gummy Fairy said, trying to sound brave.

Berry took a deep breath and knocked on the door. The door opened, and there stood a small, older fairy.

"Hello," the fairy said. She peered over her glasses to look at Berry and Raina. "Two young fairies at my door past Sun Dip?" she asked. "What brings you two here?"

"We've come for some help," Berry said bravely.

The older fairy nodded, and opened her door wider to invite them in. Her pale yellow hair was pulled back in a tight bun, and her wings and her dress were both yellow. "Come in," she said kindly.

Berry and Raina walked into the fairy's house. Berry eyed Lemona. Her yellow dress was simple and neat, and her wings were gold. She had large almond-shaped eyes that were a bright green, complementing her blond hair. She didn't look sour and mean, but Berry couldn't be so sure.

Lemona strode over to a chair near the fireplace. There was a large yellow cauldron on the fire and a plate of lemon drop candies

on a table. She stirred the pot and dropped a few lemon candies in. A poof of smoke flew from the pot. Lemona sat down in her chair and waved to Berry and Raina to have a seat on a small couch.

"What are you cooking?" Raina asked. She smelled the air. "Whatever it is, it smells delicious."

"It's a lemon broth for the candy hearts I am making," she said. She settled herself in her chair. "I'm getting too old for this!" she exclaimed as she leaned back into the chair. "Heart Day always sneaks up on me and I wind up rushing."

Berry nodded. She knew exactly how Lemona felt!

"Actually, that is why we're here," Berry said. She took a deep breath and told Lemona her story. As she sat by the fire she was amazed how easy it was to talk to Lemona. Berry wound up telling her all about Fruli and how she wanted to make a new dress. Then she explained how she had found the magic hearts.

"All the way by Chocolate River?" Lemona remarked. "My sweet sours, I have never heard of the wind carrying the seeds that far!"

"You mean this has happened before?" Raina asked. She sat on the edge of her seat, listening. This should be entered in the Fairy Code Book!

The older fairy nodded. "Yes, sometimes the strong winter winds make the seeds take flight." She reached over to stir the pot. "What did you do with the candy?"

Berry looked down at her hands in her lap. "Well, I let my friend Dash the Mint Fairy eat one," Berry told Lemona. "I know that I shouldn't have done that." She looked up at Lemona. "Now Dash is turning colors. She was yellow and now she's orange!"

Lemona shook her head. "I'm sorry to hear that," she said. "You know that candy doesn't always look the way it tastes."

"Yes, ma'am," Berry said. She kept her eyes on the ground. She was more embarrassed than ever. That is one of the first rules of candy making.

Lemona heaved herself out of her chair and walked over to the pantry. She opened up the cupboard and took out a jar. Inside were brightly colored crystal sugars, and Lemona poured a stream into the pot. "And how is Dash feeling?" she asked.

"She seems to be fine," Berry told her. "Except

her color is off. She doesn't want to be a yellow or orange Mint Fairy."

"I understand," Lemona said.

Berry couldn't believe how kind Lemona was being. When she sat and talked to the young fairies, she didn't have a sour face at all! In fact, Lemona was being so sweet that Berry started to relax.

"Those wild flavors are a bit tricky at times," Lemona finally said. She stood up to add a few more lemon drops in the cauldron.

"Can you help Dash?" Berry asked.

"I believe I know just the thing for your Mint Fairy friend," Lemona said thoughtfully. She pulled a book down from the shelf behind her.

Raina's eyes widened. She had never seen

that book before. She leaned over to get a closer look at *Sour Orchard, Volume III.*

"Will it say in there what to do?" Berry asked anxiously.

Lemona wrapped a yellow shawl around her arms carefully. "Let me just make sure," she said.

Berry glanced over at Raina. She hoped this trip to Sour Orchard would turn out to be worth their while. She couldn't bear to get another sugar fly message that Dash had turned yet another color!

Please, please, Berry wished as Lemona bent over the large book, *please find what you are looking for in there!*

9

A Peppermint Plan

Berry and Raina sat on the edge of their seats as Lemona reviewed the large Sour Orchard history book. The two fairies watched as Lemona slowly turned the pages. She stopped once to take a sip from her yellow teacup. It was so hard to wait patiently as Lemona tried to find the answer to their question. This was worse than waiting for fruit-chew jewelry to dry!

Looking around the room, Berry noticed that Lemona had many pieces of art hanging in her home. Lemona reminded Berry of her great-aunt Razz. She was a wise and beloved Fruit Fairy. Razz had pieces of art hanging in her home too. Berry never would have imagined that she would feel so comfortable in a Sour Orchard Fairy's house! She couldn't wait to get back and tell Cocoa, Melli, and Dash. That is, if Lemona could solve Dash's dilemma.

Raina looked over at Berry and smiled.

Berry was so glad her good friend was with her. "I wouldn't have been able to do this without you," she whispered.

"Oh, sure you would have," Raina said,

swatting her hand. "But I am happy to be here now. And I think Lemona is going to be able to help us."

At that moment Lemona spoke up. "Oh, here it is!" she exclaimed. She took off her lemon-colored glasses and waved them in the air. "I knew it was in here somewhere."

"Oh, please tell us," Berry pleaded. "I want Dash to be back to her normal mint self."

"It's just as I had thought," Lemona said. She peered over at Berry. "This will take some work, and you'll have to act quickly."

"Anything for Dash!" Berry declared.

"Tell us what we need to do," Raina said.

Pointing to the open page, Lemona read the instructions. "You must gather leaves from Peppermint Grove," she said. "The leaves must

be fresh from the vine, not from the ground."
She gazed up at the two fairies.

Both Berry and Raina nodded.

"Fresh mint leaves," Berry repeated.

Lemona returned her attention to the book and continued to read. "Make a strong cup of peppermint tea," she instructed. "Eat three peppermint candies from the old mint tree in the northern part of Peppermint Grove, and get plenty of rest." Lemona looked up at the two young fairies. "If she does all that, in the morning she'll wake up her own self."

Berry popped off her seat. "Peppermint tea will cure her?" she asked.

Lemona nodded.

"You'd be surprised how many ailments are cured by peppermint tea!"

Raina stood up. "I know the tree you are talking about," she said. "We'll get those things to Dash straightaway."

"Thank you very much," Berry said to Lemona. "You have been so helpful." Then she paused for a moment. "Thank you for being so sweet to us."

The Sour Orchard Fairy threw her head back and laughed. "Oh, please," she said. "We all make mistakes. I hope you've learned that you can't assume a candy is a certain way because of its color and shape."

"Yes!" Berry exclaimed.

Sure as sugar, she thought. She would never again assume any candy would be a certain way.

She pulled off two candy jewels from her dress and handed them to Lemona. "I'd like to give you something."

"Did you make these?" Lemona asked. "They are beautiful."

"Thank you," Berry said, blushing. "I'd love for you to have them. They make neat hair clips," she added.

Lemona reached out and gave Berry a hug. And Berry gave the yellow fairy a tight squeeze back.

"We must get going," Berry said. "We've got to get Dash her tea."

"Yes, it's getting late," Raina added. "We should be going."

Lemona stood up and walked the fairies to the door. "Thank you for coming," she said. "And for the candy jewels."

"Thank you," Raina said. "It really was a pleasure to meet you. Will we see you at Heart Day?"

Lemona smiled. "Of course," she said. "I love Heart Day. I'll be there, and I'd love to see you and your Mint Fairy friend as well."

"Licking lollipops!" Berry said. "We all wouldn't miss it for the world."

For the first time since Dash had taken a bite of the magic heart candy, Berry had hope that everything could go back to normal. She may not have a new dress to wear to Heart Day, but maybe Dash would be back to herself for the celebration.

As fast as fairies can fly, Berry and Raina flew to Peppermint Grove and got the peppermint leaves for the tea and the three candies. Then they quickly flew to Red Licorice Lake, where they knew Melli, Cocoa, and Dash were waiting.

"They're back!" Cocoa cried when she spotted her friends in the air. "Did you find Lemona?"

"Was she sour like Mogu?" Melli asked. "Or did she agree to help you?"

Berry looked around. There were a few peppermints giving off a soft glow to light up the area. "Where's Dash?"

"I'm here," Dash said. Her voice was muffled.

"Where are you, Dash?" Berry asked. She looked to Melli and Cocoa. Both of her friends pointed to a stack of picked licorice stalks.

"She hasn't come out of there since she started to turn orange," Cocoa told her.

Berry knelt down and peered inside the nest of licorice. "Dash, can you come out? It's just us. Raina and I have something for you."

"Will it make me return to my normal color?" Dash asked. "I'm red now!"

Melli's hand flew to her mouth. "Hot caramel," she said. "This is getting serious."

"Don't worry," Berry said. "We found Lemona, and you just need to drink some peppermint tea and eat some peppermint candy."

"All things you love," Raina added. "And we picked everything fresh from the grove. Honest." She peered over Berry's shoulder to look into the licorice nest. "Fairy Code honor."

There was a bit of rustling, and a few licorice stalks shifted. Dash's head popped out. "No laughing!" she said, her hands covering her face.

"Oh, Dash," Berry said. "I don't care what color you are, you will always be my friend."

"But look at me!" Dash cried. "I'm red!"

Raina stepped forward. "But not for long, Dash." She handed her a candy teacup of peppermint tea, and the three peppermint candies. "Lemona said to have these and then get a good night's rest."

Dash took the tea and candy from Raina and gulped everything down. She sat down on the red sugar sand and peered up at her friends.

"Do I look any different?" she asked.

"Not yet," Berry said.

"You match the sand," Cocoa blurted out.

Melli shot Cocoa a stern look.

"But I'm sure you'll be feeling like yourself soon," Cocoa added quickly.

"Lemona was so sweet, Dash," Berry told her. "She looked up the problem in a book and was so willing to help. In the morning you'll be feeling minty fresh, sure as sugar!"

Dash pulled the hood of her sweater over her head. "I hope you're right," she said. "Otherwise, there is no way I'm going to Heart Day like this."

Berry's heart sank. Heart Day without Dash? That would be awful! This peppermint plan had to work.

CHAPTER

10

True Hearts

Berry raced across Sugar Valley in the early morning light. She was rushing to get to Dash's house. She hoped that when Dash greeted her at the door, her friend would look like herself. She couldn't bear to see Dash red, pink, purple, or any other color!

The Royal Gardens were already set up for

the Heart Day celebration. From the sky above, Berry could see that the Castle Fairies were hard at work. There were small red and pink candy hearts draped from the tall sugar gates, and large heart-shaped candies hung from the royal candy trees. It was one gigantic heart fest!

Sighing, Berry hoped the day would go as she had planned. She wanted to be at the party with *all* her friends. She knew that if Dash wasn't herself, the proud Mint Fairy would not go to the castle party. And that would be all Berry's fault!

Berry raced up to Dash's door. She knocked several times. Berry was not known for her patience, and the Fruit Fairy couldn't wait a second longer at Dash's doorstep.

"I'm coming!" Dash finally cried from the

other side. As she opened the door, the bright morning light made her squint. She rubbed her eyes. "Berry?" she said. "What are you doing here so early?"

"I wanted to come see you first thing!" she blurted out. For the first time ever Berry was extremely early! She had jumped out of bed and quickly dressed. She wanted to be at Dash's side when she woke up.

"Holy peppermint," Dash said. "I don't think I've ever seen you anywhere so early!"

Berry didn't even respond. She pulled Dash out into the bright sunlight. She gasped and reached out to give Dash a hug. "You look like your old minty self!" she cried.

"Never underestimate the power of peppermint tea," Dash said, grinning. "I am feeling much better." She smiled up at Berry. "And looking much better too," she added. She rolled up her sleeves and grinned at her normal color. She was back!

"Oh, Dash," Berry gushed. "I am so glad! Sweet strawberries! This is going to be a great day!"

"But you didn't have a chance to make your heart candy or finish your new outfit," Dash said. She eyed Berry's dress. "And you're not even wearing the new dress you made."

"Don't make that sour face," Berry said, smiling. "That other dress was stained. Besides, I love this red dress. It's red for Heart Day!" She twirled around in front of Dash. "Look, I even added a sugar crystal heart here on the waistband." Berry leaned down and showed

Dash the sparkly heart she had sewn on. "I'm going to give Princess Lolli my heart-shaped fruit-chew barrettes."

"Princess Lolli will love those. And you always look fantastic," Dash said. "Even when you are rushed!" She turned back and called over her shoulder. "I'll be ready in a minty minute!"

Just as Dash ducked back behind her door, Melli, Raina, and Cocoa flew up. Each of them held their heart candies for Heart Day. Before they could say anything, Berry blurted out the good news about Dash.

"Dash is looking *so mint*!' Berry shouted. "It's truly a happy Heart Day after all."

"A day of hearts and true friendship," Raina cheered.

Berry nodded. "Thank you," she said.

"I've really learned my lesson. And I've been thinking . . ."

"Oh no," Cocoa said. "What are you up to now, Berry?"

Laughing, Berry walked over to Cocoa and gave her hand a squeeze. "I was just thinking that I haven't been very sweet to a new Fruit Fairy."

"You mean Fruli?" Raina asked.

"Who's Fruli?" Melli said.

Berry hung her head. "Fruli is from Meringue Island. She's new to Sugar Valley. Instead of trying to be nice to her, I've just been very jealous of her. And that's the ugliest and most sour way to be," she admitted.

"Is she going to be at Heart Day?" Melli asked.

"I hope so," Berry said. "I'd like you all to meet her."

Raina smiled at Berry. "You were thinking about what Lemona told you, huh?"

"Yes," Berry confessed. "I was thinking the same thing could be true about fairies, not just candies. I never took the time to get to know Fruli. Maybe she's different from what I thought."

"A perfect plan for Heart Day," Melli said.

"Yes, and the real meaning of Heart Day," Raina said.

"It's not just a party. It's a celebration of good friends," Cocoa chimed in.

"You can be sure as sugar it's a celebration!" Dash said as she zoomed out of her house. "Let's go have a heart feast!"

Together, the five fairies flew to the Royal

Gardens. There were already many fairies gathered in a line to see Princess Lolli. Lemona waved and winked at Berry when she saw her holding Dash's hand.

"Nice to see you all here," Lemona said as she flew by.

"Hello, Lemona!" Berry called out. She noticed that Lemona had put the candy jewels in her hair for the party.

"Was that a Sour Orchard Fairy?" Dash asked.

"Yes," Berry replied. "And one of the sweetest fairies you'll ever meet."

When the fairy friends joined the line to greet Princess Lolli, Berry spotted Fruli. She was dressed in a beautiful soft pink chiffon dress and was holding a cherry red heart-shaped box.

"Hi, Fruli," Berry called. "I'd like you to meet some of my friends." Berry introduced everyone and then smiled at Fruli. "And I want to apologize to you. I haven't been very nice. Please accept my apology."

A smile spread across Fruli's face. "Thank you," she said. She looked right at Berry as she spoke. "It's been hard being the new fairy. I would love to meet some new friends."

"And Heart Day is just the day for making new friends!" Princess Lolli said. She greeted the fairies and gave them each a hug. "Thank you all for coming and for these wonderful heart gifts." She looked over at Berry. "And I see you have found the true message of Heart Day already."

Berry beamed. "Sure as sugar!" she cried.

She looked around at her good friends, and her new friends. Meeting Lemona and Fruli had made this an extra-special Heart Day. No candy heart was sweeter than making new friends!

Gooey Goblins

Cocoa the Chocolate Fairy, Melli the Caramel Fairy, and Berry the Fruit Fairy soared over Chocolate River. A cool autumn breeze ruffled their wings, but they stayed their course. Nothing was going to stop them from heading to the far end of Gummy Forest.

"Look—there's Dash!" Cocoa called. As the

three fairy friends neared Peppermint Grove, they saw their tiny friend shooting up to meet them.

"You are right on time," Dash said as she flew alongside her friends. She looked at Berry and smiled. "This must be important. You are never on time!"

Berry shot Dash a sour look. "The sugar fly said Raina's message was urgent. I can be on time when I need to be!"

"And yet she still had time to put on her best sugar jewel necklace," Cocoa added with a sly grin.

"Just because I was rushing doesn't mean I have to look sloppy," Berry replied. Berry always liked to look her best and was usually sporting a new piece of jewelry that she made herself from sparkling sugar-coated fruit chews.

"What do you think this is all about?" Melli asked. She was worried about her friend Raina the Gummy Fairy. Usually Raina didn't overreact to situations. She was very calm and always followed the rules.

"Maybe she just couldn't find something in the Fairy Code Book and needs our help," Cocoa joked.

"No, there's definitely something strange blowing around the valley," Dash said. She looked back at her friends. "And no, it's not just the cold autumn wind," she added.

Melli had to agree with Dash. "This is the busiest time in Sugar Valley and we shouldn't be distracted from our work. Candy Corn Field is already full of tall stalks."

The four fairies flew in silence for a moment. They glided over Candy Castle and then they saw the tops of the Gummy trees.

"I can't wait to see Raina," Melli said. "I hope that she's all right."

"We just saw her yesterday," Berry told her. "Don't be so dramatic. I'm sure that she's fine."

Cocoa flew ahead and then called back over her shoulder, "I don't think that it's Raina that we need to be concerned about." She pointed to the south end of the forest. "Look at those trees!"

The four friends gasped as they saw the melted leaves of the gummy trees. Normally, the branches were filled with bright rainbow gummy fruits.

"No wonder she called us," Berry whispered.

"Let's go find her," Dash said.

The fairies flew deeper into the forest. There were puddles everywhere from the melted gummy candies.

"I never thought that I would say this," Dash said. "But Gummy Forest is a melted mess!" She stepped over a rainbow puddle. Even though Dash was the smallest of all the Candy Fairies, she was always hungry and was the most adventurous eater. If the melted gummies didn't appeal to even Dash, the fairies knew things were *really* bad.

"Sweet sugar!" Raina shouted when she saw her friends. "I'm so glad that you got here!"

"Oh, Raina," Melli said, rushing down to give her friend a hug. "What happened here?"

"I'm not really sure," Raina said, her voice full

of concern. "When I woke up this morning, the forest looked . . . melted!"

Cocoa, Berry, and Dash landed beside her. Their faces told Raina all she needed to know.

"It still looks awful here, doesn't it?" the Gummy Fairy asked. "The poor forest animals don't know what to make of all this. I tried my best to take away some of the melted candies and clean up some of the puddles, but that doesn't seem to be making a difference. The forest is still a mess."

"Are you okay?" Cocoa asked. She put her arm around Raina.

Raina sat down on a melted log on the ground. "I'm fine," she said with a heavy sigh. "I've been doing all sorts of research. And nothing seems to match up. All I know is that the forest animals and Gummy candies are all in danger."

"It's definitely eerie, not cheery, here," Berry muttered. "Are you sure this isn't some kind of spooky trick from Mogu?"

Raina shook her head. "I don't think so. This is really bad. Even for a tricky troll."

"I wouldn't put anything past Mogu," Cocoa said. "That old, salty troll is sour."

"Yes," Raina agreed. "But Mogu loves gummy candy. I can't see him wanting to ruin it."

The fairies all knew that Mogu lived in the Black Licorice Swamp and often came with his Chuchies to swipe candy from the Gummy Forest. The troll and his round little workers loved candy too much to spoil the crops.

Berry looked closely at the melted trees. "I think that you're right. These candies are ruined . . . even for a troll to eat."

"I told you something was going on," Dash mumbled.

Standing with her hands on her hips, Berry shook her head. "You're not saying what I think that you're saying, are you?" She smiled at Dash. "You've been reading too many Caramel Moon stories."

"Most of the stories are based on truth," Dash said. She loved to read all the spooky tales that fairies had spun about the full moon in the tenth month of the year. "Those aren't just ghost stories." Dash looked over at Melli and Raina. "Tell them!"

"Well, some of those stories are just meant to

entertain," Raina said. "But others are based on true occurrences."

Dash gloated for a minute, but then a melted candy snapped off its vine and fell on her head. She rubbed her forehead and looked to Raina. "What do you think this is all about?"

Raina plucked a droopy gummy branch off a tree. "Has anyone else seen anything strange going on in Sugar Valley?" She glanced over at Dash. "Or heard anything strange?"

"The Gummy flowers over by the Chocolate River did look melted," Cocoa told Raina.

Dash's silver wings flapped nervously. "Last night, I heard howling and moaning in Peppermint Grove," she whispered.

"Something isn't right in Sugar Valley," Melli muttered. "Oh, and there's so much to do! Think of all the fall candy crops that could be ruined."

"Let's not get our wings dipped in syrup yet," Berry told her friends. "We can get to the bottom of this."

A sugar fly buzzed up and dropped a note for Raina. She read the letter quickly and then showed her friends. "The note is from Candy Castle. Princess Lolli is calling a meeting for all of the fairies. We are supposed to go to the Royal Gardens at Candy Castle *now*."

Melli gasped and her hand flew to her mouth.

"If Princess Lolli is calling us to the castle, the situation has to be really sour!" Dash exclaimed.

"Not necessarily," Cocoa said, trying to keep her friends calm. But in her heart, she wasn't so sure. Princess Lolli was the kind and gentle ruler of all of Sugar Valley. She didn't often call a meeting with all the fairies unless something was *very* urgent.

The fairies flew off to Candy Castle hoping that all would soon be right in the Sugar Valley.

Candy Fairies

Read all the books in the Candy Fairies series!

Visit www.candyfairies.com
for more delicious fun with your favorite fairies.

**Play games, download activities,
and so much more!**

The Unicorn's Secret

Read the books that started it all!

Mermaid Tales

Exciting under-the-sea adventures with Shelly and her mermaid friends!

Trouble at Trident Academy

Battle of the Best Friends

A Whale of a Tale

EBOOK EDITIONS ALSO AVAILABLE